Pages of Love and Hate

Carol Bryant

PAGE OF LOVE AND HATE
Copyright © 2023 **Carol Bryant.**

No part of this publication may be reproduced, distributed, or transmitted in any form or by any means, including photocopying, recording, or other electronic or mechanical methods, without the prior written permission of the publisher, except in the case of brief quotations embodied in reviews and certain other non-commercial uses permitted by copyright law.

Authorunit
17130 Van Buren Blvd., Ste. 238,
Riverside, CA 92504
877-826-5888
www.authorunit.com

Because of the dynamic nature of the Internet, any web addresses or links contained in this book may have changed since publication and may no longer be valid. The views expressed in the work are solely those of the author and do not necessarily reflect the views of the publisher, and the publisher hereby disclaims any responsibility for them.

Any people depicted in stock imagery provided by Getty images are models, and such images are being used for illustrative purposes only.

ISBN 979-8-89030-062-1 (Paperback)
ISBN 979-8-89030-063-8 (Ebook)

Printed in the United States of America

Acknowledgments

It is with great gratitude that I acknowledge my daughter's Leigh, Lynn, and Faith and my sister, Diane. Forever thanks for your love and patience as I was writing this book. You have been there every step of the way, pushing when I wanted to give up and not letting me. Thank you.

I would also like to thank the professionals at Xlibris Publishing for their help with my first book. Thank you.

About the Author

I was born and raised in a small town in Canton Georgia, where I lived until I moved to Florida where I met and married my husband. I have 3 beautiful children and 9 grandchildren. My hobbies are drawing and spending time with my family and loved ones. I moved to Kentucky some years ago where I still live alone and work.

About book

The book is about meeting and finding your soul mate someone that you can be with and know that they will always be with you through it all. It's. About love and the happiness you have with your family, the hardships and sorrow of death. It's about finding out that your love is nothing more than a word, that your life as you knew it was just a lie. It's about how your husband took your love and destroyed it with cheating, lies and abuse. How you finally come to terms with the hate and hollowness that was left behind from the one person you never thought would hurt you.

Pages of *Love* and *Hate*

Maggie left the apartment before dawn; she wanted to watch the sun come up over the ocean. There was a light mist in the air. The weather channel was predicting rain and possible storm s, but this was her last day, and she needed to think and clear her head. As she walked the shore to her favorite spot, she picked up a piece of driftwood that had been washed up overnight. It had been bleached by the sun and caressed by the ocean. Its surface was smooth to touch, and the ridges had swirls. She ran her fingers over it so that she can memorize its every aspect as she can't take it with her. As she walked, she whispered into the breeze, and her eyelids fluttered as she breathed in the salty aroma of the sea. She saw white flashes out in the ocean; she stopped and scrunched her toes into the soft, damp sand.

Maggie sat in silence and watched as the fireball slowly emerged, rising on the horizon. It was magnificent; it was as though it were coming straight out of the ocean. The burst of sunlight turned the sky a soft pink, and the clouds became ablaze with the color. The waves tumbled as they struggled with the sea and crashed on the shore. They were the echo of her heart and soul and the tension seemed to melt from her body.

The light rain began to patter on the ocean, and the breeze was picking up; it was like music bouncing from within the ocean. The waves dancing as they rose and fell, they were like great mountains forever changing. And the unforgiving waves were angry, dark, and unyielding. The wind pushed against the waves, gathering in strength, only to crash one by one and never to rise again.

The breeze blew through Maggie's shirt; she bowed her head and closed her eyes from the salty sting of the waves and the rain. As she sat there, she let her tears fall. She cried for her parents, her children; but mostly, she cried for all her memories, which were nothing but pain and lies. The dampness from the wet sand already made its way through her jeans as she hugged her knees. Her hair was loose, tousled, and tangled from the light rain and the breeze, but Maggie didn't care. As time elapsed, she sat there amongst the waves and the ocean reflecting on her life. The water was warm as it crashed against the golden sand and the sun, trying so elegantly to shine in the pale sky as the gray clouds slowly cascaded across it.

A sense of nostalgia coursed through her body; it was as if she had been here forever and nothing was to be heard and no sign of hope in sight. She had flown to Naples, Florida, two weeks ago, the day after David left for one of his meetings. She needed time to think and try to come to terms with what she was about to do. She knew it was not going to be easy, but nothing had been easy in the last year.

The water was choppy, and she watched the waves as they rolled with foamy white tips, spreading themselves like the lace of a veil. They crashed with such soft sound that they were not noisy yet, but the sound was more like music of long ago. It was a beautiful sight sitting here at sunrise; there was no better place she would rather be, even in the rain. The beach was so silent. There were few birds this morning, and there were no people; the only sound was from the waves. There is a cool breze, stealing the warm th from the sun, giving me taste and smell. The ocean music takes command of my mind and ears with the crashing waves and cries of the gulls.

She took another look at the beach and looked out to the ocean, with the raindrops becoming a part of it. She can hear each watery gift; they were softer than the patter of tiny feet. The waves moved according to the wind, and she tried to commit it to her memory because it would probably be her last visit here. "Oh, how I wish I could bottle it so I could smell it and have the sound with me forever. The rain is almost silent as it touches the sand, and I think that this is how music began with its natural rhythm."

She sat there as if in leisure, forgetting everything— the time and the rain. When the clouds overcame the sunlight, she stood; and wiping her face, she made her way back down the beach. The water is rough, rougher than usual. The thick salty air consuming my breathing until it hurts. But she felt nothing but sadness as she turned and stared down the empty and lonely shore, longing for something different. Maggie had chosen the beach for her place of mourning; she needed the loud and powerful crashes to deafen her bruised and bleeding thoughts. I used to scream at the ocean but not now, now I stand in silence. She stood there watching a gateway of water worlds where the shore lay jagged and broken the outcrop just a torn piece of paper. The sea rushed forward to steal the last note of music. She had not been paying attention to the rain; she was so lost in her thoughts and memories.

The clouds that had been gathering since morning, dark and unyielding. The wind pushed against the waves not playful, but with gathering strength. The air was thick and the storm promising nothing but hardship for everyone.

Carol Bryant

As she walkes, she can hear the seagulls crying overhead; and as she closed her eyes, she can hear her mother's voice telling her that everything would be okay and not to worry. She can feel her mother's hand take hers, telling her it was time to go. As she was walking back, rain began to patter from a dark sky, and fire rose to meet them. It looked like smoke whirling around the waves and she knew dead things where being washed upon the damp and. Lightning flashed across the sky, and then a large boom of thunder came; it looked as if it were coming straight out of the ocean.

Maggie began to jog to her car; she should have left a long time ago. The wind rose and a white a storm covered the land and one by one the waves crashed but never rose again. She barely made it to the car before the downpour came; it only lasted about fifteen minutes. It had stopped by the time she got to the apartment, but she knew it would start again any minute. She was loading the car when lightning struck across the sky, followed by thunder; and by the time she was finished, it was raining again.

It had been raining off and on all day ever since she came home from the beach, and the dark clouds were building in the northern skies. It was getting dark outside now, and the rain was drumming on the roof and windows. It was much louder than Maggie would have thought possible, but her nerves could account for that. She had been nervous all day, and trying to hide it from the girls when she talked to them was almost impossible to do. How she managed that, she didn't know, but they were occupied with planning a birthday party, so maybe that explained it. They wanted to make sure she would be home for Sandra's second birthday party on Sunday. Maggie told them she would be leaving the next day and would call as soon as she got home. As she was hanging up, she told them she loved.

They had been predicting storms all afternoon, and from the

sounds outside, they were right. The thunder was so loud, and you could hear the wind howling against the windows; it was enough to give Maggie goose bumps. Crossing her arm s, she went from room to room, checking the doors and windows to make sure that they were locked. She went to look and make sure that she had candles close by in case the lights went out.

She went into the kitchen to make some hot cocoa to try to soothe her fragile nerves. She was so nervous and full of anxiety as the day rushed to an end. She hoped the storms would stop by morning because she hated flying when it was storming. All she thought about was the plane crashing. She knew it wasn't just the storms that was bothering her; it was also the fact that she would be going back home tomorrow before David got there. He would be home in two days, and she knew what would happen: he would be furious and start yelling abusive words at her. It was always the same; he would threaten her like so many other times when she had told him to leave. But this time, she wasn't backing down; she was holding on to what was inevitable. She wanted him out of her life; she had put up with enough of his abuse for two lifetimes. Now she just wasn't going to take any more; the girls were grown and had families of their own. And she just couldn't see living the rest of her life in turmoil and abuse and with his cheating.

It was always the same every time David went on his trips— well, meetings actually. He was involved with a group called the Legionnaire Club he held an office, so he was gone a lot. Ever since he became involved with the group, he had changed. They argued constantly. Nothing was ever good enough for him anymore; everything had to be his way. But this time was going to be different; she was telling him to get out and that she wanted a divorce. She had packed all his things before she left and already had them sitting by the front door, waiting for him. She knew he would be furious and threaten her again and that he'd say he would see her dead before he gave her a divorce.

Outside, it began to rain harder, splattering on the windows. The wind lashed in a torrent; it was as though it were determined to strike fear into her. She could hear every creak of the building and the trees; it was like they were screaming. Maggie usually liked the rain; she loved walking in it. She found it somewhat comforting, but tonight it sounded ominous. The rain on the windows reminded her of the tears running down her face from all the crying she had done over the past few years. A large clap of thunder startled her, and it reminded her of his fist pounding her body.

She tried watching television but couldn't pay attention to it; all that was on was the approaching storms and the newscasters telling people to take shelter. So she turned the radio on for company, but that didn't last; they just talked about the storm that was beginning to rage outside. She was just too edgy, and nothing could drown out the sounds from outside. The storms they had been predicting all day were finally here. She just hoped it wasn't as bad as they were now predicting.

Maggie finally just lay down on the bed, thinking she could rest, but the memories of happier times came rushing in on her. At around 2:00 a.m., she gave up trying to sleep; and getting up, she wrapped a blanket around her shoulders. She curled up on the sofa and watched the rain and lightning in the darkness outside. She sat there and let all the memories rush in— from the moment she had moved to Naples, Florida, with her young daughter Mandy, who was only four years old, to meeting David. The tears started, and she couldn't stop them, so she just let them fall. She cried until the sun was peeking through the clouds. Getting up, she went into the bathroom, took a long shower, and got ready for her flight; maybe she would sleep till she got to Louisville Airport.

Maggie's mind just wouldn't stop thinking about her marriage—well, her whole life. She thought about the beginning. Actually, the first time she saw David, she had been drawn to him. He was like a magnet pulling her toward him. He was tall and handsome with broad shoulders and light brown hair. He had this air about him that pulled you in, and he could always make you laugh. He had this boyishness about him that drew you to him, and he could spin a tale to make you believe everything he said. He was the kind of guy whom you never forgot, and he left his imprint in your mind. There was this casualness about him, and when he spoke, he had this accent that told you he was not from Florida. He had this perfect smile that said, "Come on, you can trust me." His voice was like sugar, sweet and luxurious. It was not ordinary; it had a richness to it that sent a warm glow throughout your body.

Maggie couldn't explain the feeling she had, but she knew that she was going to fall— and hard— for him. She never thought that the first time she saw him would turn out to be such a beautiful and devastating thing. When she first met David, she didn't want to get involved with him or anyone. She didn't have the time or energy, and she wasn't sure that she was ready for it.

She had moved to Florida to be close to her parents— as they both had health problems— and her oldest sister, Mary, and her family. They lived only a few blocks from the beach, and she loved it. She didn't like leaving her younger sister, Pamela, in Georgia, but her husband would not move and said he was not giving up his job. Besides, Pamela wanted to stay close to his parents. They had two children,

Victoria and Jeff, just toddlers, three and two. Maggie knew she was going to miss her and the kids; she was her best friend and confidant. The two of them did everything together. They even completed each other's sentences; that was how close they were.

After Mandy and Maggie were settled, Maggie started taking her and Mary's two children to the beach every day. It was the first time Mandy had seen the ocean, and she had never seen so much sand in one place, and she loved playing in it with her cousins. Maggie called them her sea nymphs. The beaches in Naples were so beautiful; the sand was soft and almost white, and the water was turquoise blue, with foamy white waves gently lapping at the shore. Every morning, the kids and Maggie would take walks on the beach; the soft sand glistened as it joyfully reflected the early morning sun rays. The sea sparkled as it strolled up the shoreline, leaving glistening seashells behind, and the kids would pick them up to make castles with them later.

Maggie's mom and dad loved to go with them sometimes; they couldn't stay in the sun for very long at a time. They couldn't walk as far as the kids did, so they would bring chairs, sit in the shade, and watch them play. They made them laugh with their antics and water games. Whenever Mandy would ask if Papa could play with her, he would say, "Are you going to try and bury me today?" She would giggle, and he would always give in, sit in the sand, and let her pile sand on his legs, telling her she was just trying to dig a hole to China. She would tilt her little head and ask him what that was.

He'd say, "Not 'what,' honey, 'where.' China is a place on the other side of the world."

She'd look at him and say, "Oh, is that very far from here?"

He would laugh, ruffle her hair, and say, "Very, very far away, munchkin. Maybe when you're older, we can go there."

You could tell her little mind was thinking, and she said, "Can Mom my and Nana come too,

Papa?"

He would look at her and say, "Of course. We couldn't leave them behind. They need to have fun and explore China too."

Every day we went to the beach, and it was always ablaze with all the colors of the rainbow. There were so many umbrellas that it was hard to see the sand. Mandy would sit there at the water's edge, her little head moving with the waves, the warm sunshine on her little body, and her fingers raking through the sand. Maggie wished she hadn't forgotten her camera, but she would remember that day forever. The gulls were singing as they flew over and around them, looking for food, as the morning wore on. The kids and Maggie had so much fun playing in the water, and she loved watching them roll in the sand. It was hilarious to watch them ; they would have so much sand on them that you couldn't tell where it started and stopped.

The sand was a golden color with the warm th from the sun, and sitting on the beach, it was like a hug from a lost love waiting for you without stretched arm s. With browning legs curled up and dusted with sand, she sat close to the lapping water's edge with Mandy. The water was so warm, and she wiggled her fingers in the water to make Mandy laugh. Scooping her up, Maggie ran into the water as a small wave came in, letting it hit Mandy. She screamed with delight and said, "Mom my, do it again."

As the day wore on, they gathered more shells and small rocks, and the four of them built sandcastles. They were deep in color like golden honey, and salt water trickled over them like a river as they poured the water over and around them, but they would be gone by morning. Maggie sat there and imagined the sand was sweet golden grains of sugar; it reminded her of Mandy's birthday cake.

Some mornings, you could see baby sea turtles, and you had to watch so as not to step on jellyfish and sea debris that washed up overnight onto the beach. And on some days, you could actually see a dolphin swimming and jumping in the water. When the sun set, it was like watching a fireball drop into the water; it was the most magnificent sight. When you looked at the ocean, it was like looking at a photograph with the warm th of the sun.

Maggie loved to take walks on the beach by herself after all the beach goers left for the day; she would leave Mandy with her parents. It gave her time to think and be one with the sea. She especially liked to go after a rain shower because the mist that swirled thick above the waves hid what was beneath the sand— sea tangles, sea urchins, and dead white sand. As she walked the shoreline, the sand shifted underneath her feet, and she listened to the lullaby of the waves. She knew the ocean was alive with constant motion and sea dwellers and knew not to go out into it at night by herself. The waves were not gentle. They rolled up the beach with their white foam overlapping; they moved with force but died within a few feet from her. The fragrance was salty, which reminded her of fishing boats and old nets.

Maggie thought this place could be anywhere the mind chose to be. The wind carried whispers and laughter on the breeze across the open sand dunes, and she thought this was nature at work. The grains of sand were still warm from the afternoon sun, and the stars were just starting to shine. It was as though Mother Nature kept them in her pocket until this moment when she was standing here alone, looking up to them. When she was looking up to the sky at night, it was like the earth and the moon had lent their warm th and light until the sun returned at dawn with its brilliance as promised. The ocean breeze and the sun had been wonderfully warm today,¬breeze was cool; it was like it was reflecting the changing moods.

Maggie watched the kids for the rest of the summer until school started back. She put Mandy in preschool and went to work at a hotel as a front desk manager. That was where she met David as he worked for a construction company that was remodeling the hotel. As she went to work that morning, she watched him walk steadily down the sidewalk. He had this air of self-confidence about him. He glanced over his shoulder, and there it was— that glance that told you he was interested. She smiled and went on her way.

Maggie shivered as she ran her hands down her arm s, thinking, That was weird. I mean, he is cute and all, but I just don't have time for men. Later that day when she saw him, there were those shivers again, and she knew she was in trouble. She would see him from time to time walking past the office; he would stop but never came inside. Every day David came by, he would look in the front door and walk away.

That evening, she picked up Mandy and the kids, and they went to the beach for a while. They were stretched out on the sand, with their arm s and legs moving to look like a starfish. They had this grin that covered their faces, and every time a wave came up to touch them, they would giggle and move their bodies faster. We had only been there for about an hour when David strolled up to them and asked if he could join them. "Of course," Maggie said.

The kids asked who he was, and she told them, "A friend. How did you know where I was?"

"Well, I kind of followed you. I wanted to give you time to get the kids settled before I came up to you," David said.

"Why didn't you just ask me before where I go in the afternoon?"

"I really didn't think you would have told me."

"You're probably right. I wouldn't have."

Mandy was not shy; she just walked up to him and asked, "Do you want to play with us? We're being a starfish."

"I would love to," David told her, "if your mom doesn't mind."

"No, that's fine, but don't feel like you have to," Maggie replied. To her surprise, he went and played with them. He rolled in the sand and jumped in the water with them on his back. Whatever the kids wanted to do, he did it.

When she told them it was time to go, David helped her pack things up and said, "I had a good time with your daughter, niece, and nephew. Maybe next time, I'll bring my daughter, Noel, if that's okay with you."

"That would be great. We would love to meet her, and she is welcome to come and play with the kids anytime," Maggie told him.

As he was leaving, he turned and said, "Thank you, Maggie, for letting me enjoy your family. I'll see you tomorrow."

Every morning David would come in to say hi and ask how things were going before he went to work. He was forever dropping into the front office to ask questions about something. "I forgot to write down what color went in the bathroom ." Just silly things like that.

As he came into the office one morning, his boss came in behind him. "David, have you lost something?"

David was startled to find he had followed him in and said, "No, just looking."

His boss cackled at him, just shook his head, and said, "Get back to work. She'll be here when you get off."

Some days Maggie had to work the night shift, and he would come into the office, sit, and talk to her. All the construction crew lived on the premises while the work was being done, so he didn't have to go far to go home. He talked about his marriage, his bitter divorce, and his eighteen-month-old daughter, Noel. David seemed very sweet, and you could tell he loved his daughter just from the way he talked about her. He carried all these pictures of her around with him. He was always showing Maggie new pictures of her that he had taken when he saw her last.

David told her he had just finished his eight-year tour in the military and had moved to Naples to be with his pregnant wife, Janie. After his daughter was born, he said Janie had filed for a divorce. She told him she didn't love him and didn't want to be married to him anymore. He said that Janie had told him she had had all the military life she could handle, that she had found someone else while he had been away, and that they had been seeing each other for a while. "I didn't contest the divorce. I figured she had cheated on me while I was serving my country, and I didn't want a relationship or marriage based on lies," David said.

David was all about the military. He breathed and ate it; he talked about it all the time. "I was shot in the leg twice, and after I healed, my team and I were sent on a convoy. We ran into trouble, and our jeep ran over a mine. It exploded, killing four of our team members. When the mine blew, shrapnel went through my legs and back. I stayed in the hospital for six weeks. I retired after that. I just couldn't take going back out on maneuvers anymore. Sometimes, Maggie, I still have nightmares of that night when we were attacked. I still see that mine exploding in front of me and my guys falling. Sometimes it's still all I think about."

David told her things about his life in the arm y and that he didn't know if Noel was his biological daughter or not. "She is mine in every sense of the word, and no one can take that from me."

He told her about his aging parents and that they were still alive and lived in a small town in Chicago, Illinois. "They live with my brother and sister. They had me late in life."

He talked about his goals and what he wanted in life. "I want to own my own construction company and build abstract buildings and do all the designs on them. I took architecture in college, and I was good at it. Before I went into the military, I had already lined up several companies to do the designs for. But all that fell through when I left for boot camp. I keep asking my boss to let me do some designs on one of the town houses that we're building. But so far, he just keeps putting me off about it."

David would come into the front office when no one was there and just talk. "You know, Maggie, I get the feeling that if we keep talking, we will end up getting to know each other better and have great conversations and be real friends. And I know we will take it to becoming lovers and then live, love, and laugh together. There is so much pleasure in true love, don't you think so? All I want is someone to love and live a beautiful long life with. Love assures us that we will never be alone, and it means having someone who will always put you first no matter what. Love comes to you softly without knowing when, how, or from where. It is simply there. Love comes to you unexpectedly, and it's there when you least expect it." He was always saying simple poetry to Maggie, and she thought he was very good at it, or he memorized it every night just so he could say something different whenever he came into the office.

They didn't see him at the beach for a couple of weeks; he was busy with the remodeling at the hotel. They had a deadline, and what free time he had, he spent with his daughter. The kids were disappointed that he hadn't been back and were always asking when he was coming by to play with them. It was lightly raining when Maggie picked up Mandy that day, and she asked her mom if they could watch her for a little while. "I wanted to go to the beach for a walk."

Her mom said, "You know it's raining, but I know that's when you like to walk. Go ahead, but be careful. And don't stay out there too long. You don't want to get caught in a downpour, Maggie."

"Thanks, Mom. I won't."

When she got there, it was raining softly, and tiny fragments from raindrops became part of the body of waves. It was so beautiful to watch and hear each drop fall, softer than the patter of tiny feet crossing the room . The sea was forever stretching, it is marked with this beautiful Apricot color that turns to Turquoise. Her narrowed eyes watches each cresting wave as it desends upon the shore. The subtle waves moved with the wind of their own accord; it was like music from different rhythms of nature. The rain turned the sand to a creamy maize, and one might think, Can anything be more beautiful than this? And she looked at the gently sloping dunes as they softly tumbled to kiss the water's edge; it was more beautiful than she could ever imagine. The gently drifting clouds were like sails searching for that lost ship; it was a rare gift from God to be able to see this breathtaking picture, and she was so glad that she was there to witness it.

After weeks of David coming by every day, he finally asked her out to dinner. "Maggie, would you like to go for a walk on the beach, or should I take you home?"

"No, I love walking on the beach in the evenings. It's perfect this time of the day."

Onto the almost white sand of the shore, gentle waves were washing and the fading sun still warm . The stars were aglow and streaked across the sky, and she said to David, "I think that the moon chooses to give us its beauty and light and the brilliance of the stars to look at forever." She breathed the ocean air deeply and listened to the waves as they came in. It was like a lullaby that went straight to your soul.

David took her hand, and as they strolled, he began to sing a love song to Maggie. His voice carried over the beach, and the few people who were still out would stop, look at them, and smile. You could hear some say, "Look at the lovebirds." But he just kept on singing. They walked up the beach to the pier and watched the boats come in for the night. They slowly retraced their path back. Before they knew it, it was going on midnight, and Maggie had to be up and at work at five thirty that morning.

As they turned to leave, Maggie turned toward the ocean; and in the twilight, the beach looked to be the color of sepia. The sand was the color of oranges and the water a darker shade of blue. Their bodies touched as they stood there taking in the beautiful picture, knowing that tomorrow it would be different. David put his arm around her and gently turned her toward him, and her lips parted as he bent toward her with the softest kiss. When he took her home, David said, "I would like to see you again, Maggie."

"You see me every day, David."

"I know. I mean, will you go out with me again? I think about you all the time, and you are always on my mind, Maggie. I feel happy when I'm with you."

"Yes, I really would like to see you again."

They started dating and spending a lot of time together after that night. On his lunch breaks, he would bring Maggie little snacks of ice cream and hot fudge sundaes, saying that she needed something sweeter than him. He always had some funny saying whenever he brought something. She always just laughed at him and told him how silly he was, but she loved every minute of it.

David was a romantic guy; he loved reading poetry to her while they sat on the beach, opening car doors, taking her elbow, or holding her hand. "It gives me so much happiness knowing that you are happy with me, and my heart is so full just knowing that you want to be with me."

Each morning he would come in to say hi and give her a quick kiss. Then one morning David came and said, "Good, beautiful morning to you, sweet sunshine angel of my life and my everything. I have a confession to make. I think I love you. A wish, being with you. A vow, your happiness. A dream, to have you eternally. An emotion, our first kiss. A goal, a life to two. One request, please love me. A reminder, I will love you always. All this because I know I love you."

Maggie was stunned at what he was saying. She had no idea he was thinking like that, and her mind just went blank. She couldn't speak. She just looked at him with wide eyes. "I know I have surprised you, Maggie, but this is how I feel, and I hope you feel something for me."

"Oh, David, of course, I feel something. It's like magic inside my heart and soul, and I know that I love you."

Her mom and dad had met him, and they thought the world of him, and they adored Noel. They were always inviting him to dinner and telling him to bring his daughter so that she and Mandy could play together.

David started going with Maggie to pick up Mandy, and occasionally, he would bring Noel. They would take them to the beach or the park and always sit in the shade so the girls didn't get too much sun. Her sister Mary and her husband, Gerald, liked David, and they got along great. Her children adored him. Mary came over to her mom's and said, "Maggie, I would like for you to bring David and his daughter over to the house tonight."

"Okay, but why?"

"Mom and Dad haven't told you yet?" Mary asked.

"Told me what, Mary? What's all the secrecy about?"

"Our brother just came down for a visit, and he would like to meet him."

"Mary, you are kidding, aren't you?"

"No, Maggie, he came down to look at some property. He's moving here."

"What about Pamela? Has she decided to move here too?" Maggie asked. "I miss her and the kids so much."

"No, not yet. She said that she would call us this evening though," Mary stated.

"Oh."

"Maggie, just a heads-up, our dear brother said he would decide if you should keep David or not." Mary started laughing at her and said, "Oh, Maggie, you should see the look on your face." Her brother, Bobby, and Mary were always making jokes and having fun at other people's expense.

Mary said, "I wish Pamela was here. We would have some great times with you and David. I hope she gets to come down here soon."

Pamela called, and they put her on speaker so everyone could talk. "Well, tell me, does Bobby like David?" Pamela asked.

"Yes, he does. And surprisingly, he gave his approval," Maggie said.

"Maggie, I'll call you the first of the week. I need to talk to you about something," Pamela told her.

Pamela called on Monday morning while Maggie was at work. "Okay, sis, tell me about David and his daughter, Noel. And does Mom and Dad really like him?"

"Yeah, they adore him and Noel, and we're moving in together this weekend," Maggie said.

"Well, I guess he must be okay for you to move in with him. I'm happy for you, sis. You deserve to be happy for a change."

As they talked, Pamela said, "Maggie, I really miss my family. I feel alone here without all of you. I can't pretend to Josh that I'm happy. He can see it on my face. Do you think maybe you, Mom, and Dad— if he wants to— could come up for a few days?"

"Let me see what days I can get off work. I would love to see you, sis, because I miss you too. I'll call you tomorrow and let you know when we are coming, okay?"

The next day, Maggie talked to Pamela. "They said I could have all of next week off. They said they would be shorthanded because two of their employees had quit but to go ahead and take off. It was their slow time, and they would manage. Mom and Dad both are coming with me."

"Maggie, are you bringing Mandy? I can't wait to see her. She has to have grown so much."

"I am," she said. "And I quote, 'I have to see Victoria, Mom my.'"

"Maggie, you won't lose your job over this, will you?"

"No, I won't. We are slow right now with the renovations going on."

"Well, I know you have to work. You didn't tell Mom or Dad that I asked you to come up, did you? I don't want them to know how lonesome it is here without them. I'm going to see if Josh can take a week off so we can come there for a visit over Christmas. He's due a vacation."

"That will be great, but in the meantime, we will see you in two days. Yes!" Maggie yelled.

As they ended their conversation, they both said, "Love you, sis."

The next day, everyone was excited about leaving, especially Mandy. She was all but jumping in her seat. "How long till we get there, Mom my? I can't wait to see Victoria and Jeff."

When they pulled up into the drive, Pamela and the kids came running out, and Mandy was screaming, "Let me out! Let me out!" It was fantastic seeing Pamela and the kids. Maggie didn't know just how much she had missed her. It seemed that the week went by way too fast, and they didn't want to say goodbye. They all were crying as they drove away. Pamela didn't get to come down that year, and they missed her and the kids. They talked to her almost every day.

Pamela called one morning. "HI, sis. Are Mom and Dad there with you?"

"Yes, they are sitting here. Why? What's wrong, Pamela?" Maggie asked her.

"Nothing's wrong. Can you put them on speaker?"

"Sure, hold on a minute."

"Hello, everyone. I have some news for you," Pamela said.

"Well, don't keep us in suspense," Maggie told her.

She laughed and said, "Everything was great, Mom, Dad, and Maggie. I'm pregnant again, and I amso happy and just wanted you all to know." They wanted to know when she was due. "The baby is due after Christmas." They asked if she needed anything right then, and she said no. They talked for a while and made plans to be there before the baby was born.

Over the months, David had become friends with Maggie's brother-in-law Gerald, and they spent a lot of time together. They both liked football, and when a game was on, Maggie and David were always over at their house.

When Pamela was seven months pregnant, she called their parents. Hysterical, she was crying so hard that their dad couldn't understand what she was saying. Her dad said, "Pamela, calmdown. What's wrong? What's happened? Has something happened to one of the kids?"

"No, Dad. Josh was killed this afternoon. One of our neighbors killed him, Dad."

"Pamela, are the kids okay? Where are they? Are they with you?" her dad asked.

"Yes, they are here with me, Dad. I need you and Mom to come to Georgia right away. I need you both so much. Daddy, please I need you and Mom now. Please come tonight, please."

"Pamela, we'll be there as soon as we can get airline tickets," her dad told her.

Her mom had been listening to a one-sided conversation and kept asking, "What's wrong?" Their dad told them, and their mom jumped up, rubbing her hands. "What are we going to do? Robert, we don't have the money for plane tickets. Our check won't be here for another week. What are we going to do? We have to get to our daughter tonight. We cannot leave her alone."

"I know, Eve. I'm thinking. Give me a moment to think. I'll call Mary and ask her if she can help. She will be devastated by Josh's death, and she may want to go with us. Eve, while I'm making calls, you go pack a bag for us, okay?"

David had been listening to their conversation and just said, "I'll get the tickets for you, Robert. No need worry." And he called the airport and made reservations for them. Two hours later, he and Maggie drove them to Fort Myers and put them on the plane. Mary didn't get to go but asked them to tell Pamela that she loved her and she was sorry about Josh.

Eve called Maggie when they arrived in Atlanta and said they would call when they saw Pamela and the kids and let them know how she was. Later that evening, her dad called and filled them in as much as he could. "Maggie, according to the police report, Josh had run over this neighbor's dog. The neighbor said he knew it was Josh because he found his dog lying on the side of the road."

"How did he know it was Josh? Did he see him do it?" Maggie asked.

"No," he stated, "he hadn't seen Josh run it over but knew it was him because he heard him when he came home. The other neighbors said he started yelling and cursing Josh as he came running down the road. The neighbors also said Josh went to park his car, and the guy with the dog came storming into the yard with a brick in his hand."

"Why didn't one of them do something?"

"I don't know, Maggie. I'm telling you what happened," Robert snapped. "They said when Josh got out of the car, he didn't get a chance to say anything. The guy hit him so hard in the chest with the brick that it ruptured his lungs."

"Oh my God, Was Pamela there? Did she see what happened?" Maggie asked.

"They told me Pamela came running toward Josh screaming, and he was bleeding from the mouth and fell down. Pamela put his head in her lap, yelling for help, crying. And Josh died in her arm s."

"Dad, how is she holding up? Is she okay?" she asked, crying.

"For now, they gave her a small sedative to calmher down."

"Did they arrest that guy for murder?"

"No. They said there would be an investigation."

"What? Are they crazy? They have witnesses of what he did!" she screamed into the phone. "The police never did anything to this man for murdering my sister's husband!"

"Said it was justified."

She asked her dad, "How could it be justified when he killed a man with a pregnant wife and two children over a dog that he didn't even know who had ran it over?"

Josh's funeral was two days later, and Pamela went a little crazy. She actually tried to take Josh out of the casket, crying, "No, no, you can't leave us!" It took three guys to get Pamela to let go of him. They had to sedate her before the funeral.

A week after the funeral, the neighbor with the dog started harassing Pamela, beating on her doors after dark, yelling insulting remarks to her. Robert would call the police; they would come by and say, "Well, did you see this person?" Because of the sudden death of her husband and the trouble with the guy next door, Pamela went into labor early. She barely made it to the hospital; she gave birth to her son Austin on a gurney before the doctors could get there. He was small but otherwise okay. Thankfully, the nurses knew what to do. She was in the hospital for a week before she could bring the baby home.

Robert had talked her into moving to Naples with them and told her that she didn't need to stay there by herself with three children. Maggie flew up to help her, and her mom pack everything up. That night, the neighbors started the same old thing, beating on the doors and windows and throwing things at the house. They knew her dad was older and that he wasn't capable of taking them on. Maggie opened the door and called out to them to leave her alone. All they did was laugh and throw another rock. Maggie called the police, and when they got there, they said, "Well, did anybody see him this time?"

She hit the roof and said, "What's it going to take for you to do something? Wait for them to kill her or one of the children? My god, she just came home from the hospital."

"Well, miss, did you happen to see the person or persons outside?"

"Yes, I did, and it was the people next door." Maggie snarled.

"Well, you will have to come with us to identify them." They put her into the back of the cruiser like a common criminal and drove her all over town.

"Why are you driving around town like this?" she asked them.

"Well, miss, we are cruising around," the second officer said.

"And just why are we cruising around? You know where they are," Maggie snapped.

"Miss, you are going to have to calm down. We are only trying to help."

"Yes, you are trying to do something, driving me around like a criminal."

Finally, they stopped and asked. "Do you recognize anyone?"

"Yes, that's them. Those three guys are the ones at the house."

They didn't get out of the cruiser or call for backup, nothing. They just took her back to her sister's house and said, "That's all we need from you, miss." Nothing was ever done to them. They didn't even question them. Perhaps the police knew the neighbor so well and they ran around together that they decided to overlook anything that he and his boys did. They never arrested them or had a trial. They said it was all circumstantial evidence, and the case was dismissed. The sad part was Pamela never had closure from her husband's murder.

David flew up to drive the U-Haul truck back to Naples for them ; it was the first time that he had met Pamela, and he tried to do everything for her that he could. Their dad and mom thought he was great, trying to do all this for them.

When they returned to Naples with Pamela and the kids, she stayed with their parents for a while until she found a house that she liked. Pamela bought it on sight and said it had enough room for her and them. "Your place is with me, Mom. Your place is too small, and I want you and Dad to live with me." So her mom and dad moved in with her to help take care of her and the kids.

She was still having a hard time trying to adjust to Josh's death. She tried to explain to Victoria and Jeff why their daddy wasn't with them. "Your daddy went to heaven so he could always watch over the three of you and me." As the weeks went by, Victoria and Jeff adjusted very well to losing their dad. David tried to include them in everything he and Maggie did, taking them to the beach, taking time to play with them. He always included Pamela and her parents in everything he and Maggie did.

David was forever wanting to go over and visit, even started going fishing with their dad. "I need to spend time with him because he is as close to a father as I have." David would take off early on some days just to go over and visit with them. Robert loved it when they came over. He liked playing pool, and he would get them together and bet that he and Pamela could beat Maggie and David. It tickled him to death to beat them. They never told him they let him win. As time went by, David wanted to spend more and more time over at their house or take all of them boating, including the kids. "Maggie, they need to get to know me and to know that I'm here for them."

Late one evening, David and Maggie went for a walk on the beach. He whispered into the breeze, "My beautiful angel, you are my life. You are my entire world. You are the one that I want to be with, you are the one that I need, you are my love, my everything. Love isn't about how long you've been together. It doesn't count the days, the weeks, or even the years, Maggie. It's all about how much you love each other every day that matters."

She closed her eyes, and she breathed in his cologne. Her toes felt the softness of the sand, and his arm went around her shoulder. Maggie wiggled as a shiver ran down her spine, and her eyes burst open. His hand massaged her shoulder, and the sand blurred as her eyes shed a tear. "I know, David. It's that love that's so strong that I feel for you."

They watched the fading shore as it turned to liquid gold with the brilliant light from the water. Ever so gently, David lifted her head; her lips parted as he leaned forward with the gentlest kiss. They gazed at each other, and with her head on his shoulder, they turned to the far-off horizon. The last of the melting sun disappeared into the ocean. It was like a painting overpowering with color but something that you can never forget. It was like the waves were the lips of the ocean, and with every crash unto the shore, it sang a rhythm of its own, soft and subtle. It was magic. It was like all the love and passion of God went into it.

David and Maggie had been together for three years, and on her birthday, he took her out to dinner. "Maggie, I want to ask you something."

"Okay, what is it, David?"

"Well, you know I love you with all my heart."

"Yes, I know. What are you trying to tell me, David? Are you leaving me? Did you find someone else?"

"No. I want to know if you will marry me." He took out a beautiful diamond ring and put it on her finger.

"Yes, yes, I will marry you. I love you," she said as she bent over to kiss him.

"I know I want to be happy, and I will do whatever makes you happy, Maggie. I can be happy just by putting happiness and joy in your life. Whatever makes you happy would give me pleasure. I will smile with you, always hold your hand, and have long walks with you, whether it's to the coffee shop, to the stores, to the movies, or to the beach as long as I'm with you."

"David, you don't have to make all these promises."

"Yes, I do. I desire my life with you just as I want to be happily in love with you. You are my angel. You give me inspiration to do my best in becoming a better man, and we can make the best life together. Honestly, if you would stand with me, I will hold your hands and never let you down. I can't wait to start my life with you, Maggie."

"David, we have shared a life together. A marriage certificate won't change how I feel about you."

"I know that, but I want to marry you to make you mine in every sense of the word. I will shower your life and our love with roses as I adore your beauty, and I'll treat you like the angel you are to me. I'm already looking forward to life with you and growing old with you. I want to stay in this life and be happily in love before I die."

"You are never going to die, David. You are so full of energy." David was so sincere, and she cried as he spoke those words, for never had anyone said so much love to her. They both agreed on a small church wedding as they both had already been married once. She wanted all the thrills and frills of a big wedding with lots of flowers and food, even though they were only going to invite sixty people.

One night they were by themselves. Mandy was spending the night with Victoria. They got to talking, and Maggie asked David, "You seem very knowledgeable about women. I mean, you know what to say at the right moment and what they want. I know it's a little late asking, but just how many have you been with to learn all this?"

He looked at her and said, "Maggie, does it matter? I'm with you now. But if you must know, I've only been with two women, a girl in Vietnam and my ex-wife."

"You are joking, aren't you? I mean, there is just no way you have learned all that with only two women."

"It's the truth. I went into the military when I was seventeen. I had been dating Janie when I went to boot camp. I married her on one of my leaves before I was sent to Vietnam ."

They set their wedding date for April 11, and they were going to have both of their children and Victoria stand with them. Maggie had seven months to prepare for her wedding day; even though it was small, there was a lot of work involved in it. She could only do things on the weekend and make calls through the week. Eve, Pamela, and Mary helped her plan every detail, even helped her pick out the flowers and the food to serve. Her mom told her, "Maggie, your father and I are going to pay for the cake as one of our gifts to you."

"Mom, you don't have to do that. We can pay for it all."

"No, we want to do it."

"Okay, you pick it out, Mom, whatever kind you want." She didn't think she would pick a large, four-tier cake. So they all told her that it was way too much for the small service they were having and that a smaller cake would be better. She wanted a tiered cake, and they couldn't change her mind. So the cake designer told her she could do a smaller, three-tier version of the one that she liked. That satisfied her, so they ordered the cake and the flowers for it.

They went shopping for dresses and found three just alike for the girls but had no luck finding what Maggie was looking for. For weeks, they went shopping for her dress and just couldn't find the right one. Then they went into a little out-of-the-way boutique, and there on a mannequin was the dress she wanted. It was simple but elegant; it was off-white satin with a short train, and it fit perfectly.

"Maggie, you need a veil," Pamela said.

"No, I don't want a veil; and I didn't want one. I'm going to use baby's breath instead."

When they were hunting dresses, David and the guys were hanging out. "All we have to do is show up in a suit. We don't have to look good like you do," David said. "Believe me, no one is going to be looking at us." ALL eyes are going to be on my four beautiful girls.

Their wedding day turned out to be perfect. There were no clouds, and a light breeze was blowing. The church was beautiful with flowers everywhere, even down the aisles, and more than the few people they had invited attended. The girls were the most beautiful and precious things as they walked down that aisle in front of Maggie, each one holding a nosegay of tiny pink and yellow flowers. They seemed so grown-up at that moment, each one taking turns kissing her and then David and saying "I love you." They were giggly, and all three wanted to hold Maggie's bouquet, so they each had a hand on it. At the reception, David danced with each of the girls, waltzing them around the floor, and he even danced with Pamela, much to Maggie's surprise as she didn't care for him.

After the reception, the couple left on a short honeymoon as neither one of them could take off from work for more than a few days, so they went to Disney World for four days. Maggie had never been there, and that was where she wanted to go. It was everything people said it was; it was magical. You could be anyone from anywhere, and no one cared. All that mattered was seeing things you could only imagine. They went around the parks with Mickey and Minnie Mouse wedding attire on their heads, but they were not the only ones dressed like that. Everywhere you looked, someone had the same thing on and having a great time. It truly was magical.

She had not been that happy in a very long time, and David made sure that they saw and did everything in those four days. Maggie told him they would have to bring the girls back to enjoy the magic and see all their favorite characters before school started back. All he said, laughing at her, was "Okay, honey, anything you want."

She leaned toward him, and he met her halfway with a big sloppy kiss, licking at her face. She tried to dodge him, but he caught her in midstride. She was laughing so hard that she bent double. People looked, laughed, and kept on walking, smiling at them.

In July, they took the girls, her mom and dad, and Pamela and her three kids to Disney World. They had the time of their life. Maggie had never seen her mom and dad laugh so much and enjoy everything around them. It was like watching two kids experience the joys of life for the first time. They all, especially the kids, had the greatest time watching shows and parades and all the characters go up and down the streets. They even managed to get signatures from most of them ; it was a special time for all of them.

For the first three years, everything was great. That was until Maggie became pregnant, and David changed before her eyes. She thought he would be happy about the fact that they were going to have a baby. Maggie knew she was. She wanted Mandy to have a sister or a brother to play with, even though Mandy and Victoria were as close as two sisters could be. And it was a fact that Noel didn't get to spend a lot of time with them.

David wasn't around very much through her pregnancy, so Pamela stepped in to help Maggie with everything. She helped her pick out the baby furniture that David said he didn't have time for. They had so much fun buying baby clothes and folding the tiny sleepers and outfits. Pamela went with Maggie to all her doctor's visit, and when she asked David to go to the Lamaze classes with her, he wanted to know why. "Why do you need me for that, Maggie?"

"Never mind, David. I'll get Pamela to go with me. The doctor said we needed the class, and I just thought you might like to go." She didn't ask him to go again.

Pamela and Maggie had a great time decorating the baby's room . Everything was in off-white and pale pink. David finally did go to a couple of classes with Maggie, and he was there when their daughter was born. She was so tiny and perfect with dark brown hair and green eyes, and she had a tiny, little heart-shaped mouth; she was so beautiful.

Later that day, when the nurse came in with the baby, she placed her in Mandy's arm s, which Maggie had asked her to do. Mandy opened her little eyes so big, smiled, and said, "I'm your sister." Then she looked over at them. "You think she can see me, Mom my?" They had decided on a name for her, but Mandy wanted to call her Carrie, so that was what they named her.

Over the next few months, it seemed things were going good between David and Maggie. Every afternoon he would come home and help her with the kids. When people came over, he would come up to her and put his arm around her. He would say he had four beautiful girls, and he didn't know how he became so lucky. David would then kiss her; everyone would laugh and tell him, "Man, you have a beautiful wife and family."

When the new wore off of people telling him how lucky he was and what a perfect life he had, he started coming home late a couple of nights a week. This went on for weeks, with him staying late at work. It went from twice a week to every night of not coming home. "I'm sorry, but we had trouble at the jobsite." Every day was a different excuse. "Sorry, the boss made us work overtime. One of the guys got hurt." It became an everyday thing that he worked overtime, never coming home till around eight o'clock or later at night. "Maggie, I'm sorry, but the boss decided we needed to finish up this project we are on. We are supposed to start another one in a couple of weeks, so I will be working late every night."

"I thought that you weren't allowed to work nights at that property, David."

"I told you I was sorry, Maggie. Get off my back about it."

"I am not on your back, and don't raise your voice to me, David." All I did was ask you a question. You have told me something different every night. What are you talking about I have told you the truth why I am working late every night. I'm sure you are I just don't know which excuse to believe. Believe which ever one you want to, they are all the truth,David snapped." It was just Mandy, Carrie, and Maggie lately; he had been so distant since Carrie had been born, never wanting to be around. He made so many excuses, staying gone as much as he could. And when he was home his mind was somewhere else.

Mandy would come over to Maggie when she was feeding Carrie and say, "She's still small, Mom my, like my baby doll, see?" She would hold up her doll and try to measure them, and they both would laugh.

When David came home early on occasion, Mandy would go to him. "Daddy, will you play with me?"

"No, Mandy, I don't want to play. Why don't you go to your room and play by yourself? I'm tired, and I just want to sit here and relax."

Her little head would drop, and she would come over to Maggie.

"Mommy, he's grumpy and doesn't like me anymore."

Maggie would just hug her close and tell her, "He loves you, honey. He's just worked hard today, and he's very tired." It made her want to smack him up beside the head; it was as though he didn't see the hurt on her little face. "What if I play with you and let Daddy rest? Is that okay with you?" She would bob her little head up and down with a smile on her face. They played board games and Barbie dolls, whatever she wanted, while he sat there staring out the window.

David didn't get to see Carrie or Mandy grow because he was never home after those first couple of months. He didn't hear Carrie's first words or see her first steps; he didn't even notice her first tooth. He never came home before she was asleep. Maggie never knew where he was; he wouldn't say. But in the back of her mind, she knew he was cheating on her; he was never dirty when he came home supposedly from work.

One night she just asked him, "David, why are you gone all the time? You never spend time with the kids, and you haven't brought Noel home in over two months. So what's going on?"

"Maggie, don't start. You know I have to work, and sometimes I work overtime. You do remember we have a family and a baby to feed."

"Yes, David, I know we have a family and a baby to feed. But when are you going to be a father to them? Carrie is over a year old, and she doesn't even know you. You haven't even noticed that she's walking."

"I have been busy, and I know how old she is. I was at her birthday party, wasn't I? Look, Maggie, I was there when she was born, and I live here, don't I? I'm the one who gets woken up in the middle of the night from a crying baby and still goes off to work before daybreak."

"Yes, David, you do, and so do I, but do you hear me complain or stay gone all the time? No, I'm here for our children and their wants whether it's at 9:00 p.m. or two in the morning. That's what parents do for their children."

"No, that's what you're for, Maggie, not me. I go to work, and when I come home, I want to relax, and I can't do that here. It's just too damn noisy around here, that's why I go somewhere quiet. They are just too loud, and I just can't take the noise. Sorry, that's how I feel."

"You are self-centered. Do you know that? What gives you the right to ignore our children when all they want is a little attention from their father?"

"Call it what you want, Maggie. I don't care."

"David, we don't wake up with perfect thoughts or perfect lives, but you can't keep ignoring the children. That is unfair to them." That was when things started to go sour in their marriage. He stayed away even more. Never giving an excuse where he had been or with whom, he just didn't care.

About six months later, he started coming home on time. "You know, we need to spend time with your parents, Maggie, and the rest of the family," David said.

"Why now, David? You haven't wanted to go over with us in a long time. So what has changed your mind about going over there?"

"I've been doing a lot of thinking, and I just miss seeing them every day, okay? Besides, I have joined this private club for veterans. It's called the Legionnaire Club. It's a group of veterans that help each other. It's where you can go and talk to people who have been in the military, and they know what you are going through, how rough it can be when people don't understand you. It's a place where I can be myself. And before you ask, yes, it has a bar, but it is for members only. And you had to have been a member of the military and in good standing to belong."

"How come you are just now telling me that you joined this legion?"

"I just didn't think about telling you until now."

Something had changed him. Maggie was not sure what, but he started coming home early every day. He would bring Noel home to play with the girls; he even helped out with the chores around the house. "David, why are you home more now than you were two months ago?"

"Well, I have been talking to some people, and they told me I needed to be more understanding. They said I should help you with the family, that I couldn't just hide from my responsibilities."

"Oh. Who did you talk to, David?"

"Oh, just some of the guys I work with and some of the guys I know at the club. We can talk to each other there, tell them our problems, and we don't get judged for what we say."

"So what, are they your shrink now? Do you tell them what's going on in our personal life?" Maggie snapped.

"No, Maggie, I don't. I don't have to tell them anything. They know just by looking at me that something's not right in my life. Let's not argue. I want to go over to Pamela and Mom's house to check on them. I haven't seen them in a while, and I miss talking to your dad and mom. How's Pamela doing?"

"She's okay."

"She hasn't been over in a while unless she comes while I'm at work."

"They are all fine. If you came home occasionally, you would know that. The kids and I go over every day for a little while to check on them."

David wanted to go over there every afternoon, saying, "Maggie, we should try and take care of them and help Pamela as much as possible."

"Look, David, I love my parents and my sister. I like spending time with them. They are my rock. But spending every afternoon there until ten or eleven o'clock at night is not right, not for them or the girls." She couldn't understand why he wanted to go over every evening. "We need to stay home and not be a pest staying that late."

"Why do you say that, Maggie? They love having us over. Don't you see the joy on their faces? They love watching and playing with the girls."

A year went by with them going over to Pamela's house, cooking, playing in the pool, going to the beach, and watching the kids grow. Pamela had started dating again, and she was becoming like the old sister Maggie knew, grew up with, and loved. David had not met Kevin, and he didn't like him when he met him that evening. "She can do better than this Kevin guy. I don't like him." He was always putting him down, and perhaps Pamela had listened to enough.

They went over one afternoon, and David started the same thing, telling Pamela she needed someone different from Kevin. She stood up and, right in front of everyone, said, "David, if you can't say something nice about Kevin, then keep your mouth shut. This is my home, David, and I will not tolerate you insulting my guest. I will invite whomever I want to. I don't ask your permission on anything that I do. You do not tell me who I can or cannot have at my own home. And if you don't like it, then maybe you should stay at your own home."

"I apologize, Pamela. I'm sorry for overstepping my boundaries. I just want what's best for you and the children, and I promise I won't say anything else." Pamela just gave him a look, and if the look could kill, he would have died on the spot.

It had been about four months after the blowup at Pamela's when he came home one afternoon at around one o'clock. David came in with alcohol on his breath and the smell of stale cigarette on his clothes. Maggie had just picked up Carrie from day care; she wasn't feeling well, and Maggie had just laid her down for a nap. Mandy was at Eve's. She loved going over to play with Victoria every day; those two were inseparable. David came into the kitchen, where Maggie was putting away the groceries. He was slurring his words. "Well, Maggie, what have you been doing all day, out playing the queen?"

"I have been taking care of errands before I go back to work tomorrow, and what's with this queen thing? David, where have you been, and why aren't you at work?" Maggie asked him.

"I went to have a few drinks with some of the guys at work. We were celebrating John's divorce. Where are the kids? I don't hear them."

"Carrie is asleep. She wasn't feeling well, and Mandy is with Mom. What do you mean John's divorce? He just got married two months ago."

"Yeah, well, I guess his wife didn't take her vows literally. He caught her messing around on him."

"I'm sorry to hear that, but it's no excuse for you to skip work and go get drunk."

"What do you know about it, Maggie? You sit in your ivory tower and think everything is just great. You don't see the outside world for what it is."

"I work outside the home too, David. I don't sit in what you call my ivory tower. I have to work just like you. Only difference is I come home to my family and take care of them. That's more than you do."

David turned, went into the living room, and yelled, "Maggie, come here!"

"Keep your voice down, David, so Carrie doesn't wake up. I'll be there in a minute." She wasn't fast enough because, the next thing she knew, he had her by the arm and twisted it behind her back.

"I told you to come here. When I tell you something, Maggie, you better listen. And what was that crack about me not taking care of my family? You know that's a lie. I work every day to put food on that table of yours," David slurred.

"David, let go of me. You're hurting me." She tried to get her arm free, but he just twisted it more. He started ripping at her shirt and tore it off; he began pinching and twisting her body. He grabbed her breast and twisted them so hard, and it hurt so bad that it brought tears to her eyes. She could feel the pain all the way to her toes. She finally got her arm free and pushed him away, and she tried to go around him. He grabbed her by the hair, yanked her backward, and threw her on the floor. The coffee table went sideways when her head hit the corner of it, and she saw stars. She slapped him across the face and kept pushing at him. "David, get off me and leave me alone."

He went crazy, yelling, "You don't tell me to leave you alone, bitch!"

"I am not a bitch." And she slapped him. She was fighting him, trying to get free of him using her legs to try to dislodge him from sitting astride her. She can't budge him, and he was still yelling at her as he was pulling at her clothes.

"You belong to me, and I'll do whatever I want to. Do you

understand? I own you just like I own everything in this house!" David yelled. Maggie could hear Carrie crying upstairs; he had woken her up, yelling. David held her down with one arm across her throat. She was swinging her arm s and legs, trying to hit him. She can't catch her breath; he kept pushing down on her throat. She kept fighting him, and he ripped her pants off.

"David, get off me!" she was yelling as she tried pushing him. She can hear Carrie screaming at the top of her lungs for her from her room, and there was nothing she can do. She can't get to her. It was as though David can't hear Maggie or Carrie. It was like some demon was within him. The rougher he was toward her, the better he liked it. Maggie tried to convince herself that it was the alcohol talking and making him the demon attacking her. But somewhere in the back of her mind, she knew it was him.

David raped her on the living room floor not once but twice, holding an arm across her throat. "You wanted it, and you know it. That's how whores want sex, rough and violent. You got just what you wanted," David slurred. Her throat was so irritated from yelling, and with his arm across it, she can barely swallow. When he finally rolled off Maggie, it was all she can do to move and stand up. Her body was already bruised from his pinching her. She had small cuts on her arm s, and where her head hit the table, there was blood running down the side of her face. She was so cold, and she felt like vomiting.

As tears streamed down her face, she felt shame and self-hatred because she failed to stop him. She started to tremble as she tried to make it upstairs to put on a robe before going to Carrie's room to check on her. She had cried herself to sleep, and she had her tiny fingers in her mouth. Maggie went into the bathroom to take a hot shower and to see how much damage he had done. The whole time, she was praying that David would not come in. She didn't think she could have stood to look at him.

She hid the bruises on her face with makeup, and the cut on the side of her head had stopped bleeding, so it was easy to hide. But the sad part was he intentionally violated her and made her feel ashamed and guilty. She felt so dirty, cheap, and humiliated that she started to cry again because she was utterly helpless against a drunk.

She got dressed and put some clothes for the girls in a bag and went downstairs. David was still lying on the floor, passed out, and she left him there. She put the bag in the car, went back in, picked up Carrie, locked the house, and left. The kids and Maggie stayed at her parents' house that night. She never told them what David had done because her dad would have killed him. She hid the bruises from them with long sleeves and pants.

When she went home the next day, she asked them to watch the kids for a little while because she had to take care of some things. "Mom, I will be back later to get them." She called into work and told them she was sick and would be in the next day. What she should have done was call the police and have him arrested, but she was too ashamed to even do that.

Maggie was waiting on David when he came home that afternoon. She had bought a baseball bat and hidden it in the closet. She didn't want guns in the house because of the kids. When he came in, he started crying when he saw her. "Maggie, I'm so sorry. I don't know what came over me. Please forgive me. I promise never to drink again, but you have to believe me, I'm so sorry for what happened."

"It's going to take a long time for me to forgive you, David, for what you have done to me. But one thing is for sure. You lay another hand on me, and I swear I'll kill you. You intentionally made me a victim. You made me feel helpless and ashamed. I didn't ask to be raped by you, and I didn't deserve to be treated that way. It's one thing to be attacked by someone you hate or don't know, but this... this was something different, David. This was the kind of hurt and humiliation that could only be inflicted by someone you love whom you thought loved you. I have cried because you hurt me, but then I realized that I hurt myself believing that you would never hurt me like that. I wish everyone could know what kind of person you are, but they would just turn it around on me as my fault. And I know it would hurt the kids, and I will never let my children know the humiliation that their father has put me through.

"David, I didn't make a mistake by loving you. I didn't even make a mistake by giving you a chance. I made the mistake by trusting you, believing in you. The mistake was yours. It was your choice to not respect me and to hurt me. It was your mistake that you thought so little of me that you humiliated me and made me feel so dirty and unwanted. You violated me, and you violated my rights as a person. And what I should do is call the police and have you arrested for rape."

"Maggie, I beg you, don't do that. It would cause so much trouble with my job, and it would give Janie an excuse not to let me see Noel. Please can't we work through this, Maggie? I can change. I know I can with your help."

"It's that very reason, David, that I haven't called the police yet. I'm not doing this to save you but not to hurt the children with their father in jail for rape."

"Maggie, you are my angel and the love of my life. I'm asking you to never doubt my love for you, and if I could take away the hurt I inflicted on you, I would. I'm so sorry for what I've done to you. I just want you to know that you are the reason I look forward to the next day, Maggie. Please I will get down and crawl and grovel at your feet, whatever it takes, for you to forgive me.

I know that it was the alcohol and me talking to the guys about all we had been through in the arm y. And when John came in and told us what had happened, it just got to me."

"Life is like that, David. It's tough, and if you give in to temptation, then yes, it's a hard lesson learned."

"I promise never to drink again. Did you tell your parents what had happened yesterday?"

"No, that is between you and me, David. I will not put them in the middle of this."

Maggie stayed with him, even though she wanted to leave, but she had nowhere to go. She couldn't afford to rent a place and take care of the kids on her salary. And she was not going to ask her sister if she could stay with her and their parents; they had enough to deal with. She wouldn't let David sleep in their room . She told him to take the spare room and that she would not sleep in the same room with him.

Six months went by, and true to his word, David didn't drink, and he came home every afternoon and played with the kids. He acted like the man she married. He was gentle and considerate and went out of his way to be nice to everyone. And one night he came to her. "Maggie, can I sleep in your bed?" She knew she should have told him no, but she reached over and turned the covers down for him. He took her in his arm s. "I love you, Maggie, so much, and I promise never to hurt you ever again. I want your trust and your love back. Please don't hate me forever."

"I don't hate you, David. You just broke my trust," Maggie said.

"I know there is no happiness for me without you, and I don't want to live without you. You are my life, the reason I live and breathe. You are my angel and the love of my life. You are my soul mate. You are so special, and I'm so grateful for everything because you are in my life."

"I love you, David. I can see the person you are. And I know the person you are. You are the one that hurt me."

"Maggie, I love you. I'll always love you. Please let me show you I'll be the man you married."

He still wanted to go over to her parents' house but not every night; he had decided that they should try to rebuild what he had torn apart, and they tried to rebuild their marriage. Once a week, David brought Maggie flowers and took her out to dinner. She knew he was trying to win her love back, and she fell for all the lies.

Eight months after she let him back into her bed, she found out that she was pregnant. She was happy about it, ecstatic really, and so were the kids. She thought that David would finally get his head straight and be a father. And he did for about a year. He wasn't there through this pregnancy any more than the first one. But he came home on time and helped her out occasionally.

He tried to include Pamela in everything he did, asking her and Kevin to come over to help him set up the crib. He asked them what paint color they thought would look good in the baby's room . He tried to be nice. The trouble was Pamela didn't like him, and she wouldn't tell me why. Maggie let it go for the time being. She was trying to get ready for the baby and just never gave it much thought.

Amy was born during a bad storm , and things were not going well for Maggie. She was scared, and that made it even worse. She was in labor for twelve hard, grueling hours. When Amy finally was born, she was so tiny and she had an almost black head of hair and big brown eyes. She was the most beautiful thing lying in Maggie's arm s, and she looked at her and said, "So you didn't want to make an appearance, did you, little one?" Maggie thought she looked just like Mandy and Carrie, and she was so proud to call them her girls.

When Amy was born, David acted like he was on cloud nine,

bragging to everyone that he had five beautiful girls now. He would come home and help with the kids; he even helped clean the house. Then one day he came home in a foul mood, yelling at Mandy and Carrie, telling them to go to their room and stay there. Maggie didn't know what was wrong with him; his mood swings were getting to her. She knew he wasn't drinking, or she couldn't smell it for one thing. She asked myself if it was possible he was on drugs, even though she could not find any in the house or the car. No matter what they did, David found something to fuss about; there was always something wrong. Nothing they did was ever right for him.

He always wanted to go over to Pamela's house. "We need to keep an eye on them because

Kevin is just not right for her, Maggie. I don't like or trust her boyfriend. There is something that just isn't right."

"Mom and Dad like him, and that is good enough for me, David. Kevin treats her and her children with respect. He does things with them. He takes them places and tries to be a father figure to them."

"Well, I still don't like him." He acted like they belonged to him.

Over the weekend, they all decided to go to the beach. They packed lunches and blankets, even umbrellas for the baby and Maggie's mom and dad. When they got there, Maggie looked at the sea; it was forever changing and stretching, leaving its mark. It had the beautiful color of apricot, and farther out to sea, it was a magnificent turquoise. She closed her eyes halfway and watched as the cresting waves descended on the shore.

The kids were already at the water's edge, playing in the waves. Carrie had her pail and shovel, digging. Mandy and Victoria went off on their own down the beach; they thought they were too old to play with the little ones. "Mom, we're going to go watch them play volleyball. Is that okay?"

"Yes, Mandy, but you two stay together." All the kids were around their age, but Maggie would keep an eye on them. It was like old times— everyone laughing, playing in the water, and enjoying one another's company; even David seemed to relax and enjoy himself.

When Amy was six months old, David received a call from his dad. "David, I'm sick, and I need you to come home. I know you have been away from here a long time, but, son, I need you. I have a job lined out for you and a place to live. I know, son, that I'm asking a lot from you, to give up your job and everything you have worked for down there and move back to Kentucky. David, I'm dying, and I want to spend what time I have left getting to know my grandchildren. That's something I should have done before now, and for that, I'm truly sorry. I can't leave your mother helpless. You know she has never worked or done anything."

So just like that, David decided that they were moving to Kentucky. "Maggie, my dad has never asked me for anything. And if that is his last wish, then we are moving to be near him before he dies. He never asked me if I wanted to move, just tells me what we are going to do. It will be a blessing to get away from all the pitfalls here in Florida. I want to be close to my family so that I can help ease the burden of Dad dying. I've been gone a long time, Maggie, and besides, I will be getting away from all the alcohol and drugs."

All at once, it hit her: he had been doing drugs. He had been lying to her all this time. He found it easier to lie to her than tell the truth. And with each lie he told, it just became a habit to him. "You lied to me, David. All this time, you lied to me, telling me you were not doing drugs. What else have you lied about? When you told me you loved me, was that a lie too? Because when love is real, it doesn't lie, cheat, or pretend. It doesn't hurt you or make you feel unwanted. It's supposed to be a cure to your worries. So has all this been just a lie, David?"

"No, Maggie, it hasn't been a lie. I loved you when we married, and I love you now with all my heart. It's always been unconditional love between us. Yes, I used drugs, and I hid them from you, but I haven't used them in months, and I ask you to understand why we are moving. It's not just to get away from easy liquor and drugs. It's also because my dad needs me, Maggie, and I don't want him to die asking that we come to him. Please try and believe in me. I want what's best for you, and I know I'm asking a lot from you to leave your family, but just stand with me on this. That's all I ask. I hate my job, and I hate this life we're living. I'm tired of always wanting what I can't have."

"What is it you want, David, that you don't already have?"

"I want peace, Maggie, something that's not here."

So Maggie agreed to move with him, leave her family, and move to this god-awful place in Kentucky. She cried every day for months; it was the isolation that she hated. His dad had found this farm for sale, and he had put a trailer on it for them. It wasn't great, but they had a roof over their head. When they moved into the trailer, there were no lights and no running water, and the job he had gotten David was with an Amish contractor. David thought it was great and said they could live like the Amish people did. "Maggie, they live every day without power and running water. They just use generators to keep their food cold."

"No, David, there is no way I am living that way, and neither are the girls. We will be on the next plane back to Naples, Florida, and if your dad wants to see them, then he can just come there."

His dad told him that he was not going to put up with any kinds of foolish thoughts like that, that he had not asked him to come home just to have the girls and Maggie leave, that he wanted what was right for them, and that David better get to his way of thinking. "I did not intend for your family to live like that, and you better listen to what I'm saying to you, son." He gave him no choice about it, but Maggie still hated it. She had completely forgotten what it was like to live in the country.

Country life is quiet. You don't hear cars or trucks roaring down the street. Your neighbors, if you can see them, don't play their music blaring. The peace and quiet of country living is what you hear when you go outside. You hear the birds singing in the meadow and the cows in the pasture.

Maggie had forgotten how nice it was to lie in the grass, watch the shifting clouds, and try to make out figures in them. You could lie out at night, and all you see are stars for miles and miles. There is no smog or pollution, and there are no skyscrapers to take away the beauty of the countryside. The beauty of it can take your breath away. Your neighbors are all close knit, and they watch out for one another. Your children can play outside, and if they get dirty, no one thinks anything about it. The children are taught how to help around the farm, mending fences, feeding the livestock, and working in the garden. Country living is what you look out your window every morning to see. It's what the city people drive for hours to enjoy. It has fresh air and blue skies. And you can bet when you walk down the street, you will meet someone you know, and they will always ask how you are.

But the girls and Maggie had no way to go anywhere; they only had one vehicle as David sold their other car before they moved. David said, "If you need something, call my dad. He can take you wherever you need to go." Well, she needed to register the girls in school as it was to start in three weeks. She needed to go to the grocery store. She needed to go to places that you didn't want to ask someone else to take you.

David went to work every day for the Amish contractor. "It's time for me to commune with nature. I really like how they think and live." David came in one day and said, "Maggie, you really should try to be more like the Amish women. You might learn a few things." He was trying to be Amish. He let his hair and beard grow; they were so long that he put both in a ponytail.

Maggie had had enough of his Amish perks. "David, either you shape up or the kids and I are gone, and I mean it. I am tired of this bull, and I amtired of always having to ask your dad to take me somewhere that I need to go. You have one week to get me a vehicle. I am tired of waiting and depending on someone else." The next week, he had one delivered to the farm ; it wasn't new, but it would get her where she needed to go.

He finally did trim his beard but refused to cut his hair. He kept it pulled back; it really was awful looking. He had no hair on top of his head, just what was in the back and around the sides. He wore a baseball cap to cover his baldness. It really wasn't nice of Maggie to laugh at him ; she just couldn't help it.

They had been in Kentucky for about five months when Maggie's parents decided to come for a visit, and they fell in love with the farm . They wanted to know if they could stay with them for a while, so they moved in with them. It was tight, but we got along great. Her mom helped with the meals, and her dad would go off into the woods. He would wander around the farm . Some days, he would take Carrie and Amy and show them the deer and the squirrels, telling them they had to be very quiet, or they would scare them away.

Her dad had been out walking around one day, and he came in and asked David, "Son, what are you going to do with the backwoods?"

"Nothing right now, just let it be."

"Well, what would you say if I asked you if I could build a small log cabin back there?"

"I think that would be great, Dad. I can get some guys to come out here and clear a spot out and build whatever you want."

Her dad loved the woods and hunting, and since they owned this fifty-acre wooded farm, he could go out and spend time in the woods. He would go out early in the morning, come back around lunchtime, and sit outside with the girls. Maggie would catch him watching the woods with an expression of longing, like he was missing something important. He had something on his mind, and you could tell it was eating at him. When the men came to clear the spot for the cabin, her dad showed them where to go. They were going to use the falling trees for the logs.

Robert never took a gun with him when he went into the woods alone. So Maggie asked him, "Dad, how can you hunt without a gun? I mean, you go into the woods every day, yet you don't kill anything."

He just laughed at her and said, "Try it sometime, Maggie." She finally figured it out: it was the solitude that he hunted and wanted, not the animals.

Her dad became very ill and was having trouble breathing. The doctor told him he needed thinner air; the air in the mountains was just too heavy for him to be able to breathe. So they had to move back to Florida for lighter air, and he never got to build his log cabin that he wanted. The doctors in Florida told him that there was nothing they could do for him and that thinner air wasn't going to help him. They told him he had a liver disease and that he only had a short time left.

They moved back to Kentucky and brought Pamela and the kids with them. Two months later,

Mary and her family moved up to Kentucky. "You are not living in some place without us close by." Their dad had told them that he wanted to die in peace and in the country, not in some hospital on a beach.

Six months later, he died from a massive heart attack; they tried open-heart surgery, but there was just too much damage done. They couldn't save him. The sad thing was their dad died in a hospital in Louisville, Kentucky. He had loved the woods like Maggie did. They were dark and lovely, like our souls maybe. But when the color of the leaves changed, so did our spirit. It was lifted, knowing that the first snow was not far away. Maggie thanked God every day that he was able to enjoy and spend his last days where he wanted to. She would never forget the smile on her dad's face the first time he came in from walking in the woods; it was like he had finally come home. And no matter how old she is she stilled missed her father.

Three months after her dad died, they lost David's father. He died in his sleep. And Maggie was glad that he was able to spend time getting to know his grandchildren.

Eve had a hard time adjusting to Robert's death, but every day became easier for her. She lived with Pamela and the kids, and all of them would take her to places that she had wanted to visit when their dad was alive. He never forgot about the cabin, and he asked David to build it before he died. They were trying to make up for all she had lost, and they wanted her to experience all the things she wanted.

Five years later, she became sick. Pamela and Maggie took her to the doctor. They were told that her kidneys were shutting down and that she would need a kidney transplant. She had already had two heart attacks, and they were scared to death. She had to start dialysis three times a week because there was no kidney available. It was so hard for them to have to watch her struggle with that; they actually removed her blood and then filtered it back in.

Pamela and Maggie went to school to learn how take care of her at home because dialysis was draining her. She just couldn't withstand the pressure of it; she stayed tired all the time and wasn't able to do much. For two years, they took care of their mom at home. They split the days up so that they could take care of their family. For the last six months, she kept going down and having problems with everything.

The week before Thanksgiving, she woke up very sick and passed out. Pamela could not wake her. After about ten minutes, an ambulance arrived, and off they went to the hospital. Eve had had another heart attack, and it was bad; the doctors couldn't do much for her and told the family to just be there for her. Pamela, Mary, and Maggie sat in a hospital room holding their mother's hand, telling her how much they loved her. They did not stand alone, but what stood behind them was the most potent moral force in their life, it was the love and guildence of their mother. She died from a massive heart attack and kidney failure. Her body was frail and holding fluid, and it made her heart flood, which caused the heart attack. She never regained consciousness and died the day before Thanksgiving. It was the hardest and saddest holiday Maggie could ever remember. Thanksgiving just became another day to her. It was no longer a holiday that they celebrated.

Never was David there for Maggie during this ordeal. She was still trying to cope with her father's death and her mother's illness. Then to lose her like that was almost too much to take. She wasn't sleeping or eating; all she did was cry. And through it all, the only thing David ever said was "I need you take care of this, if you can get your head out of the clouds. Maggie, they are gone and in a better place hopefully, so just get over it."

Her hand came up so fast, and she slapped him so hard that his head went sidewise. "Don't you ever say anything like that to me again, David. My parents meant everything to me. I loved them very much, and I miss them. Just because you don't feel their loss doesn't mean I don't. It's not my fault that you never cried when your dad died. It's not my fault that you don't feel the loss of him. There is no greater love than the love of your parents and your children, David. And when you lose one of them, there is no greater loss than that. You feel hollow because part of you is missing, and I guess we are just that much different from each other. I feel the loss, David. I know they are gone and that I will never see them again."

David never said a word to her about them after that; he became distant and started going to the doctor to get medicine. He said, "It's because of the loss of your parents, the loss of my dad. I keep thinking about Vietnam and all the things I did over there. I think about all the death and the killing, of all the bombs exploding and bullets flying past my head, and I'm wondering if it is my time to go. That's why I'm seeing a shrink, Maggie."

One night David came home acting funny. The girls were already in bed, and Maggie was getting ready for bed when, all at once, David grabbed her from behind. He put his hand over her mouth and ripped her gown off. She started to fight him like a crazy person. He overpowered her and threw her facedown on the bed. He held her head face down on the pillow so that she couldn't scream. She was trying to get away, and he grabbed her by the hair, pulled her back, and raped her from behind.

The pain was so bad that she thought she would die, and she couldn't scream because he had her head buried in the pillow. She was having trouble trying to breathe; he was pushing her head deeper into the pillow. She was still trying to get away from him, and she was crying so hard, thinking, This can't be happening again. She can feel something warm on her legs, and she knew it was blood from the violation he was inflicting back there.

When he stopped, she thought he was finished, but he just flipped her over, and she started fighting him even more. He put his hand over her mouth, and when she bit him, he drew back and backhanded her across the face. He leaned down and whispered in her ear, "Keep fighting me, Maggie, and I swear you won't see tomorrow or the girls again."

"You go to hell, David."

And he slapped her again. "Don't you ever tell me to go to hell, Maggie. I have been there, and I made it out."

For the second time in their marriage, David raped her; and the whole time, he kept her hands over her head and his mouth on hers so she couldn't scream. She continued to cry, and her tears were flowing down her face. When he had finished, he rolled over, took her with him, and cuddled her in his arm s, saying, "Stop crying, honey, and go to sleep. Everything is okay now."

Maggie thanked God that the kids didn't wake up to see what their father was doing. David wouldn't let her get up; he held her beside him all night. She must have slept because, when she woke up, he was gone; it was still dark outside. She took a hot shower to try to get the smell of him off her. She must have used a whole bottle of soap and all the hot water, yet she still felt dirty. She was ashamed for what he had done to her. She let down her guard, and her husband raped her again. He abused and intimidated her in every way possible. She was sore, and she hurt all over, but she put on a smile for the girls.

She opened every window in the bedroom, even though it was cold outside, and stripped the bed. She threw everything away— the sheets, the pillows, even the blanket. When the girls left for school, she scrubbed the entire room, trying to rid it of his smell. She used so much cleaner that her fingers were raw, but at least it was clean.

David didn't come home that night; he had his mother call. "Maggie, David said he was staying in town tonight and that he was sick and wasn't feeling well. He didn't think he could drive out to the farm and that he would be home the next day."

"Mom, tell him that we don't need him and that he needs to stay there for a couple of days. If he is sick, I don't want him around the girls."

"With him sick and all, you are right, Maggie. That is a good idea. He has been in bed all day, and he hasn't eaten anything. I tried to get him to go to the doctor because he may have a cold, but he said he was fine and just needed to rest."

Maggie said, "That is fine. The girls and I would be okay. We don't need him."

She had shut the windows earlier; it was getting colder outside. Fall had been in the air for weeks, and it had always been one of her favorite seasons. She loved watching the colors change, and some of the trees still had leaves on them, but they would fall off eventually. Everything changes, some for the best and some for the worst.

Maggie did a lot of thinking while David was at his mother's house, and she had decided to take the girls and leave. It was the weekend, and the banks were closed. He had taken the checkbook, so she would have to wait till he came home.

Later that day, the first snowflakes started to fall, and the girls were having a ball trying to catch them on their tongue. The first fall of snow is not only an event but it's also a magical event where you go to bed, but you wake to find yourself in an enchanted world. When snow falls, Mother Nature listens; it's a time for new beginnings. The snow was just a dusting on everything when they woke up; they were calling for more the next week. I wonder if snow loves the trees and fields, it covers them up snug with a white quilt and says go to sleep my darlings till spring comes again. It was how I felt I wanted to sleep until spring so that I could forget the pain.

The girls asked when their dad was coming home. "He will be home today sometime. Why?"

"No reason, Mom. It's just he's been over at grandmother's all weekend. Is everything okay with you two?"

"Girls, your father was sick, and he didn't want you to catch what he had. And to answer your question, yes, everything is good between us."

When David finally came home three days later, he was very quiet and said they needed to talk. So after the girls were in bed, Maggie said, "David, you need help. I don't know what's wrong with you, but I am not letting you get away with raping me again. I'm calling the police in the morning and report this to them. I don't even want the girls left alone with you for fear of what you might do to them."

David just looked at her and said, "Don't call the police, Maggie. Just take me to Louisville to the veterans hospital and admit me to the psychiatric ward, please. I know I need help, and I'm admitting it. I know that there is something wrong with me, and if I don't get help, I'll do something awful. So hate me if you want to, but please just take me there and leave me."

And that was exactly what she did. They kept him for four months, treating him for post-traumatic stress disorder (PTSD). They said he was so bad that she needed to come in and talk to his doctor about him. They told her that she was going to have to watch him and make sure that he stayed on his medication and, if she saw him acting weird or funny in any way, to bring him back to the hospital.

When they woke the next morning everything was covered in a thick blanket of white, paw prints crisscrossed each other around the yard. The trees were brown the only color, a vivid snow cap on top. The start of winter was like a gift, the air cold as the girls ran outside to make snow angels.

Sure the snow was pretty and fun as long as you didn't have to drive on it. Icicles dangled from the shadowy trees, each one like an ominous sword. The river frozen solid was covered with ice so thick it showed reflections like a mirror. The sky is grey and the chills sliced through the air.

The wind howled, and wisppered as the snow piled in drifts, as the numbing air kissed her face. Icicles glistened like winter daggers, and ice crystals sparkled on the roof tops it was beautiful. If she had to describe her house, she would describe it as an ice castle, for everywhere you looked was icicles sparkling like diamonds.

That morning the woods were filled with brittle silence. There was a shriek from the trees as a branch was breaking under the sheer weight of ice. Cold licked at her face and crept under her clothes spreading across her skin. With her teeth chattering she pulled her coat closer around her, her breathe was a vapor of white. Her body heat was disappearing with every step she took, the biting cold chilling her fingers to numbness as it seeped to toes and feet.

The gloom of the winter day crept into her like dampness seeping into her heart. Even the bird song comes from deep in the woods, from under the Grey sky came a steady fall of snow. There is something beautiful and special about the snow it reminds me of my parents, of how it was their favorite time of the year.

They sent David home again, and every couple of months, they would put him back in, keep him for a few weeks, and release him. They said he was very depressed and suicidal and that Maggie shouldn't leave him alone. "Well, if he is that bad, you keep him. I cannot watch him all the time. Why release him if he is that bad? You should keep him, not release him."

This went on for months, and he was making her life miserable, and every so often, she would catch him with a smile across his face. She knew then that he was faking his illness. You can tell when some people are lying; they won't tell the truth because that takes courage, and a liar is just a coward looking for the easy way out. That was David; he didn't want to admit what he was doing, so he just took the liar's way out. He lied to Maggie, he lied to the doctors, and he lied to himself just so he didn't have to answer for the abuse and violations that he committed on her.

When David came home after the fourth hospital stay, he said, "Maggie, I want to sell the farm . I want to move to town so we can be closer to my mom and the hospital." He never spoke of what happened, and he never apologized for what he did to her. Maggie agreed to sell the farm ; she had grown to hate it even more. It had so many bad memories that she was glad to get rid of it. They sold it to a neighbor who had been trying to buy it from David for over a year; he owned the adjoining farm and wanted to put his farm back together. David had never mentioned this to Maggie, and she wouldn't have known if her neighbor hadn't seen her at the store. It was just another one of David's forgotten lies. They sold the farm to their neighbor, and he told them to stay there till they found another home. Maggie thought that was very nice and considerate of him.

They found a nice old Victorian home close to town and bought it; it had a few acres with it and a large building close to the house.

David said, "I think this will be nice, don't you think, Maggie? It's close to the hospital in case we need it." David had been going back and forth to the veterans hospital for PTSD for over a year, talking to them about Vietnam and going back to when he was in the military. They had put him on some medications.

One night after they had gone to bed, Maggie woke up, and he was standing beside the bed with this look on his face. She started to speak to him, and he jumped astride her. With both hands, he grabbed her around the throat and started choking her. He was telling me that I should have died a long time ago. She can't breathe, and everything was starting to go black when her hand found the lamp on the bedside table. She grabbed it, swung for his head, and made contact. He let go and fell to the side of the bed.

When Maggie could breathe, she moved to turn on the lights. She didn't see any blood, so she knew he was not hurt to bad. He moved, sat up, looked at her, and said, "Maggie, you hit me. Why did you do that?"

"Because you were trying to kill me, David. You were choking me."

"Oh, Maggie, I'm sorry. I didn't know it was you. I was dreaming and thought you were one of the guys in Vietnam . You know I wouldn't hurt you on purpose."

One day when he thought Maggie wasn't watching him, he overdosed on his medication. Luckily for him, she saw what he did, and she knew he had done it on purpose. She took him to the hospital and told them what he had done, and he was sent back in. He stayed there for three more months.

While David was in the hospital, Maggie opened a small flower shop in the building beside the house to pay the bills and buy food for the girls. School was out for the summer, which was great. She didn't have to try to buy clothes for them. All three went and got a summer job to try to help her. She told them that they didn't have to do that, that everything was going to be okay. "But if you are going to work, then put your money up so you have it for school."

The flower shop did really great. Maggie worked there day and night to make it one of the best in the area. It was posted in the papers as the best place to go for all your floral needs. It became very popular in town, and she even had people from other states calling and asking if she could ship orders to them. It carried them through some very rough times as David never went back to work when he came home from the hospital. He received a pension from the military, and he drew social security disability benefits. For a while, he helped her out with everything. Then he would go out and spend money on stupid stuff and then sell it for less than what he paid for it. He would tell people that she made him sell everything and that he had to pay for the girls' car and everything that they wanted. He lied to everyone he met who would listen to him.

When Maggie started a catering business along with the flower shop, David thought that was a great idea. He actually helped her a couple of times, and then he would get tired of working and go back to the veterans hospital. "Maggie, I just can't take being around people like that. My nerves and body won't take all the hassle of working like that." So she did it with the girls' help, and then Pamela started working with her.

They were busy in the floral shop, and they were doing catering jobs every weekend; it seemed everyone wanted to book an event with them. The reviews were great, and they had people booking two years in advance. The business was doing great, and it put all three girls through school and college. They helped Maggie, along with their friends, during the summers, and they never asked their father for anything.

And then a friend asked Maggie to do her daughter's wedding and reception at the Legionnaire Club. She said that it was a club for veterans and active military and their spouses only. She said that her mom and dad belonged to it. David decided to help them that night, and he met a few of their members. He was asked to come back and join when they found out he was a veteran. They told him it was exclusive. It was the same kind of club that he had joined in Naples, and Maggie asked him not to join, but he just ignored her like she wasn't even talking.

He joined that club and started going there every Monday night, at first, to help with bingo. Then he started going to the bar, which was supposed to be for members only— so Maggie thought. He would come home and tell her that he only had a soda, knowing that she could smell it on him. After four years of going by himself, he came in and asked her if she would come and help them out on bingo night. He said they needed help, and since she wasn't working on Monday nights, they could use her to walk the floors. He made sure to tell me that I wasn't allowed to go downstairs to the bar.

One night after a Thursday meeting, he came home and said, "I was asked to run for commander of the legionnaire Club. I need you to stand behind me on this, Maggie. I know I've been sick and not helped you very much, but this is something that I want to do for me. Nobody knows that I've been in the hospital, and I want it kept that way, understood? And if I become commander, I will be traveling a lot, and you won't be able to go with me all the time."

"Well, who said that I wanted to go with you, David? It's fine with me. I love having time for myself and the girls," Maggie retorted.

David became commander of the Club and while he was on one

of his many trips, Mandy became engaged, and she asked, "Mom, will you do all the wedding for me and help me pick out my dress?"

"Oh, honey, I would love to."

She picked the flowers she wanted, and Maggie made sure every detail was perfect for her. Her dress was made of white satin and lace, and it had tiny inlaid flowers all over it with a long train. She wore a short veil so as not to hide the back of the dress. They decorated the church with flowers and harps; they had candles sitting everywhere. Mandy asked her sisters to be bridesmaids along with two of her very close friends.

On the day she got married, it started to rain in the morning. She said, "Oh, Mom, it's raining. What will we do?"

"Mandy, don't worry about it. It's just your grandparents telling you they are with you."

By the time of the wedding, the rain had stopped, and the sun was shining brightly. She was breathtaking. David had taken the time to walk her down the aisle and be there for her.

When she became pregnant, Maggie was so excited. She told her, "My first grandchild. I can hardly wait." They had a ball shopping, and when Danielle was born, Johnathan was out of town, and Maggie had to be Mandy's coach. Maggie cried when she saw Danielle; she was so tiny and perfect. She looked just like her mother with dark brown hair, the cutest little mouth, and big brown eyes. And when they placed her in my arm s so that I could take her to the nursery, Maggie cried again. One of her greatest joys was to watch her granddaughter being born.

Later that year, Maggie decided to stop working all the time, and she cut her hours back and hired someone to help out in the shop. She wanted to spend time with her granddaughter.

Three years later, Mandy gave birth to their grandson Jared; he was this cute little chubby thing with reddish-blond hair, and he looked just like his dad. When he was two years old, Mandy and Johnathan were divorced, but they stayed friends. Johnathan spent a lot of time with his son and tried to help out as much as he could. Jared loved his dad and enjoyed talking to him. Jared would spend every weekend with his dad; it was a good time for both of them. Mandy made sure that Jonathan got to spend as much time with his son as possible.

Johnathan was on his way to watch Jared play a soccer game, and he was talking to his fiancée when a semitruck ran a red light, hit him broadside, and killed him instantly. Jared had a very hard time trying to adjust to losing his dad, and Mandy and her fiancé Darren had to take him to therapy twice a week. Maggie hated the thought that her grandson was having to go through this ordeal at such a young age. But she knew Darren loved him and had always treated him like his own son, just like he treated Danielle like his daughter.

And through everything that their grandson was going through, not once was David there for him or Mandy. The deep pain that is left at the death of a loved one is something absolutely and irretrievably lost. And David was just too busy with his new life and friends to even notice the agony that Jared was going through. David had been voted in as commander of the Legionnaire Club for a second term. "Honey, we need to move so that I can be closer to my club. I amgoing to have to spend a lot of time there now, getting used to running it like a business," David said.

"David, what amI supposed to do with my business? Just close it?" Maggie asked.

"Yes, that's what I'm telling you. You don't have to keep working seven days a week, Maggie, and you can work from home and only do the jobs that you want," David said.

"Why didn't you run it like a business before?"

"Because I was getting used to all the ins and outs of the place, Maggie. There is a lot I have to know." He put their house up for sale, and it didn't sell right away, so they rented it to a couple and bought a house in Spurlington, Kentucky.

Carrie and Amy both were still living at home, and when Carrie became engaged, she asked, "Mom, would you do my wedding? I'd like for it to be similar to the one you did for Mandy. I would love for you to do the catering, but I don't want you to work it, or should I get someone else to do it?"

"Carrie, I will do the wedding and the food for you. I will hire someone to help with it. You, my darling daughter, will not have someone else do this for you." So rubbing her hands together, Maggie asked her, "What kind of wedding are we doing?"

"I want an evening ceremony, Mom, with just candles in the church and piano music. Is that okay with you?" Carrie asked. "I just don't want a lot of fuss and you working on it that much. Besides, you have to help me with my dress and everything else."

"What about the cake? What do you want?"

"Well, I saw this picture of what I want. It's a tiered cake with candles and crystals around it. It's really pretty, Mom," Carrie said.

"Okay, I'll take care of it, honey. Show me the picture of what you want," Maggie said. So together, they planned every aspect of her wedding right down to the color of napkins.

It was a beautiful wedding with candles and draped chiffon on the pews, and they put candelabras all across the front of the church. With the lights turned down and the piano music playing, it was just breathtaking. It was exactly what Carrie had wanted.

Two years later, Amy was getting married, and she wanted Maggie to do her wedding too, which she loved doing. "So, baby girl, what are we going to do for this wedding? I think something different, don't you?" Maggie asked her. It was different. She wanted flowers and lots of them. Maggie put flowers outside the church, down the aisles, and all across the front of the church. They were everywhere, and it was fabulous. People were taking pictures and saying they had never seen anything like it and wanted to know who had done it.

A lady came up to Mandy and asked her who had done the design for the wedding. She replied, "My mother. She does all the designs on weddings and the catering. There is nothing she can't do or wouldn't do for her daughters, and she does the best work of anyone."

Maggie never asked David to help her with anything concerning their weddings, but he took all the credit. After Amy's wedding, Maggie closed the flower shop and stayed at home for a while. She wanted to relax and enjoy some of her life. She had been working nonstop for years, and she was tired.

Amy came to her one day and said, "Mom, I'm going to have a baby."

Well, that just tickled Maggie. She said, "Finally, another baby I can spoil." When her daughter, Sandra, was born, Maggie was there with her and Craig through it all; and when she got to hold this tiny little creature of pink, she cried. She had a headful of dark hair and a little pouty mouth; she was beautiful. Maggie would go every day and see them, and when Amy went back to work, she babysat her granddaughter for her.

One year later, Carrie and her husband, Thomas, came in smiling. Maggie asked, "What's going on, you two?"

"We're pregnant, Mom. So what do you think?" Carrie asked.

Maggie just jumped up, grabbed both of them, and said, "It's about time. When are you due?"

"In December, about a week after Sandra's first birthday," Thomas said.

"Well, you planned it pretty close. They can grow up together and be best friends."

Carrie's daughter Brandy was born three weeks early, and she had to be flown to a children's hospital because she was small and having trouble breathing. Carrie and Thomas never left their daughter's side; they stayed with her day and night, until she was able to go home. Two days before Christmas, they were able to leave the hospital with their daughter. Brandy was the best Christmas gift anyone could ever receive.

When Maggie's girls did something, they went all out because it wasn't two years later that Amy gave birth to her second grandson, Jason. What a chubby little thing he was with red hair. He and Sandra were like night and day. Amy had to go back to work, so Maggie volunteered to watch both of the kids for her, and it was a job, but oh, how she loved it. She could spend time with all of them, and it kept her busy.

When Sandra was four, Amy decided to put them in a day care. Maggie argued with her and told her she liked watching them. Amy said, "Mom, you have had them since they were born. Now it's time for you to take a break. They will be fine there. I know everyone that works there, okay?"

So Maggie was back to having nothing to do except hang out with friends. That lasted for maybe two months when she was asked by the board members of the Legionnaire Club to work at the bar for them. At first, it was just to work as a fill-in when the regular bartender wanted a day off. Then it went to two days a week and then four days. And finally, they just fired the gentleman who had been working and said the bar was making better profits with a woman working.

At that time, she did not know anything about bartending. She did not have her license to tend a bar. So she took bartending classes and passed with a 99 percent, which was high for a first timer who had never worked in or around alcohol before. She received her certificate, and she was so proud of her accomplishments.

The girls took Maggie out to lunch that day, and David had to come along. "Congratulations, Mom. This is for all your hard work." And they gave her a cute bag with every kind of tool you could use at a bar.

She thought David would be happy for her too, and it was a letdown when all he said was "Well, congratulations, Maggie. You finally accomplished something."

The girls looked at their father, and all three spoke at once. "Is that all you can say to Mom, Dad? We think it's great that she did this for herself and finished in the top of her class. Not too many can do that."

David didn't say anything, just rolled his eyes at them. Perhaps he thought it would defuse the tension he had caused. But Carrie took care of the tension before the others could say anything. Carrie said, "Mom, Dad, I have an announcement to make. Thomas wanted to be here, but he couldn't get off work."

"Carrie, what's going on?" Maggie said.

"Well, you know that we have been trying to have another baby, right?" They all nodded. "Well, we tried and tried. And finally, it happened. I'm pregnant and due toward the end of September." They all started talking at once, telling her how happy they were for them. "I know this was your day, Mom, but I just couldn't wait any longer to tell you," Carrie said.

"Honey, there is no better time than now to tell me this great news. Congratulations," Maggie said.

David looked at her. "Can you two afford to have another baby, Carrie? I mean, look what happened to Brandy. She had to go into the hospital for weeks."

Carrie looked at him with tears in her eyes and said, "It's not up to you, Father, whether or not we can afford this child. We have never asked you for anything, have we?"

"David, you apologize to her right now. You had no right to say something like that to your daughter," Maggie said.

"Carrie, I'm sorry. It's just I don't want to see you guys having financial trouble, and besides, I thought you were looking to buy a house," David said.

"We were, but the house can wait. There is nothing wrong with where we live now," Carrie said.

"Well, what if this baby has the same problems with her lungs as Brandy had when she was born? What then, Carrie?"

"Then Thomas and I will deal with it just like we deal with everything else. Don't worry, Dad, you won't be inconvenienced," Carrie said.

When the girls departed and it was just David and Maggie, she turned to him. "You bastard, how could you sit there and say those things to Carrie? She will never forget what you said, and neither will I. You are so heartless and cruel."

He just looked at her and said, "Well, it was the truth. They don't need another kid to feed."

On September 19, Miss Candice made her appearance; she was a healthy and beautiful baby. She had an unruly dark mass of hair like her sister. Maggie would stand at the window, look at her, and tell people, "That's my beautiful granddaughter."

Carrie only had to stay two days in the hospital with the baby, and when she came home, Thomas decided that she should stay home with the babies. Carrie called her boss and told him she was taking a leave of absence to stay at home and take care of the kids. Carrie would come over with the babies and spend the day with Maggie and talk nonstop, but Maggie always hated it when she left; it meant she was alone again.

David came home from one of his doctor's appointments. Maggie was in the kitchen when he walked toward her. "Oh, Maggie."

"What's wrong, David? Did you have a wreck, or did you kill someone?"

He started to cry. "No, I didn't do either. They told me today that I have lung cancer and that I have less than two years, maybe less. They said that I needed to get my affairs in order before I became too ill."

"David, I'm sorry to hear that. Is there anything that I can help you with?"

"Yes, I want you to be here for me through it all. I don't want to die alone."

"You will not die alone, David. You have me and the girls. You will have to tell them that you have cancer."

"I don't want them to know right now, Maggie. It's all new to me. Let me get accustomed to it first."

Two months went by with him never being sick. He was still drinking and going on his trips. "Why aren't you sick and losing your hair from chemo and radiation?"

"I guess I forgot to tell you I'm not having them. They said it wasn't going to help, just make me weak and sick, so I decided not to have them."

"Why? They can prolong your life by months, maybe even a year or longer."

"I am not taking them. I don't want to be sick. Besides, I have too much to do and still enjoy myself."

It was the week before Thanksgiving that he came in with a smile on his face. "Honey, you know how much I love you and that I would do anything for you. Well, when the doctors told me to put things in order, I thought of you first."

"Whoa, stop right there. What are you talking about? You have never put me first, David."

"Anyway, you remember Adam, my friend, the guy who has been taking me to the veterans hospital?"

"Yeah, so what does he have to do with this conversation?"

"I gave you to him today. He is going to take care of you when I'm gone."

"What? What do you mean you gave me to him? David, you can't give me away. You have to own something to get rid of it."

"I know, sweetheart. And see, that's it. I own you. I have from the day we got married."

"Oh, no, you don't own me, David. You're married to me, and that's all."

"Maggie, try to understand I'm only trying to help you. Adam and I have talked about this, and he agrees with me that you need someone to take care of you."

"I don't need or want you to fix me with a partner, David. I think I'm smart enough to find one on my own if I choose to."

"Maggie, that's not going to happen. I gave you to Adam to be his woman, and that's all there is to it."

"No, that's not all there is to it. You don't own me. I am not a piece of furniture that you give away at your convenience. I'm your wife, and you can't just walk in here and say something like that to me David."

"I own you, Maggie, the same way I own everything else around here, and I can do whatever I want."

"You jerk, do you think you can come in here and announce something like that and expect me to thank you? I don't know what you are thinking, but you leave me out of it."

He walked toward her and grabbed her by the shoulders. "Look, Maggie, I am not going to argue with you about this. You belong to me, and I will give you to whomever I want to, understand? Now Adam is outside waiting for me. Do you want to come out and say hi?"

"How about you and he just leave because I belong to no one, not you and certainly not Adam . If and when the time comes, I will decide if I want another man in my life, not you."

"Why don't you think on it for a while, and you will see that I'm right? He'll treat you nice, I promise."

"Go away, David, and take him with you. I really don't want to even look at you right now."

"Now, Maggie, is that any way to talk to your dying husband?" David laughed as he walked out the door.

Maggie was so fighting mad that she could strangle him. I don't know where he gets the nerve to tell me that he owns me and then, in the same breath, tell me he gave me away. The man is completely crazy if he thinks I will go along with him.

Adam was standing by the car when David came out. "Well, how did it go? Did she agree with it?"

"Hell no, she didn't, but I'll wear her down to my way of thinking."

"David, she will fight you on this. You do know that, don't you?"

"Maggie will do what I tell her to do, Adam . She always has. She is a pushover. She doesn't like confrontations."

"Did you tell her that I was married and that she is just my lady and that I will take care of her? I won't divorce my wife for anyone. I have too much invested in it, and I am not going to lose it."

"We didn't get that far, Adam . She looked at me and told me to leave."

"David, I think you are going to have a problem on your hands."

When he came in later, Maggie was still in the kitchen. He walked up and put his arm s around her and tried to kiss her neck. "Stop it, David, and get your hands off me. You have no right to touch me."

"Honey, what's the matter? I only want to do the best I can for you."

"Keep telling yourself that, David, and maybe you can convince yourself that it's the truth." She walked out of the kitchen, went to her room, and called Amy to see if they were still coming over later.

"Hi, Mom, we thought we would, if you aren't busy."

"No, I'm not working tonight. What time will you be here?"

"In an hour. Is that okay?"

"Yes, I will be waiting. Can't wait to see my babies."

Christmas was only a few weeks off, and Maggie put the tree up for the grandchildren, and she started wrapping their gifts. She wasn't going to tell the kids that she was leaving their father over the holidays. She didn't want to ruin it for them.

On Christmas morning, all the kids showed up for breakfast, and they stayed busy for an hour, cooking for all of them, but they had a great time laughing and playing games with the new toys. And when it was time for them to leave, Maggie asked them to stay, even though she knew they couldn't. She knew they had other places to be, and it was sad to watch them drive away. She didn't want to be alone with David. After the kids left, he went to his room and stayed there the rest of the day till evening, talking on the phone. Maggie was glad that he never came back downstairs.

On New Year's Eve, the Legionnaire was holding a dance, and she had to work it. There was around a hundred people, and they were having fun blowing horns, shaking noisemakers, and wearing funny hats. At midnight, everyone started hugging and kissing one another, wishing everyone a happy New Year; and David was right there in the middle of it, drinking and being very loud.

When they went out to leave, he got in her car because he was too drunk to drive home. When he got in, he put his fist through her windshield. "You are nothing but a whore, Maggie. You flirted and kissed everyone in the damn bar. No wonder I went for something softer. At least they don't prance around like the whore you are. Take me home," David said.

Maggie didn't say a word to him. She just put the car in gear and drove. She thought, Home— it has such a nice sound to it. A little thought and a little kindness are worth more than all the money, yet there is no home to go to.

When she got there, she went into the garage. He grabbed her arms so tight, and when she turned toward him, he swung his fist. She tried to duck, but he caught her in the eye, and then he started yelling at her. She snapped. She just lost it. She shoved him away from her, and she got in his face. She started yelling right back at him. She had totally lost it. She put her hand through the garage wall; her knuckles were bleeding, and she didn't even realize it. "David, I am not putting up with any more abuse from you. If you don't get some help, so help me, I will have you committed to the mental ward at the hospital," Maggie said.

David just laughed at her and said, "You and who else? No one can do anything to me, Maggie. I'm more powerful than the president. Do you think that the club would let you get away with something like that? Get real. I can do anything and not be held accountable for it, even murder, my dear. You remember what the doctors said. I have PTSD and don't know what I'm doing, so you just remember who is running this show around here."

She turned and, with her hand over her swelling eye, went upstairs to her room and locked herself in. This wasn't the way she wanted to live. There was nothing between them but hate; there wasn't even friendship left between them anymore.

The girls came over that weekend, and Maggie tried to hide her black eye and bruises but couldn't. And when they saw her face, they all spoke at once. "Mother, what happened to you?"

Before she could say anything, David jumped up and said, "Well, her foot slid off the top stair, and she fell before I could get to her."

"Did you go to the doctor?"

Again, he answered for her. "Yes, she did, and nothing is broken. Right, honey?" David said.

"Yeah, right, nothing broken." She was broken in every sense of the word, but she would not tell her children what their father was doing to her. She just couldn't make him out to be the monster that he was no matter what he did.

Maggie had to work the next day, and there was no hiding the bruises. David was sitting there when a few of his officers came in and took him to the side. "David, we saw you bust the windshield, and we see the bruises on Maggie. So to keep things from happening, you need to go back to the hospital for a few days. Man, we don't know what happened, and we don't want to know, just take care of this."

Adam took him to the hospital, stayed with him, and brought him back two days later. "David, did you get new medication for your angry outbursts?" Maggie asked him.

"Yes, I'm on new meds, so everything is fine," David replied. No "I'm sorry" or "I'll have your car fixed, Maggie." He just went to his room and got on the phone.

David came home from one of his three-day trips and announced to me, "Maggie, I am leaving on a trip to Florida for a week, and I will be taking a friend with me."

"Who are you taking, David, or do I have to ask?"

"I'm taking a friend, and that's all you need to know, Maggie. I need you to go cash a check for me so I have plenty of money. I don't expect them to pay for anything since I asked them to go with me."

"David, I will not take this much cash out for you to squander on one of your female friends."

He got in her face and said, "You will do what I tell you to do, Maggie. What we don't spend, I will bring back, okay? Nancy and I both need a vacation. I have been working very hard lately, and I need to relax and enjoy myself."

"Nancy. You're taking Nancy. David, you know that she is a lesbian. She doesn't like men."

"Now that is where you are wrong, Maggie. She likes both, but we are only going as friends on this trip."

Maggie was looking forward to some time away from him so she could try to figure out what she was going to do. David made sure that he kept all the money, even hers, that went into the account. She knew he wasn't spending all that he was taking. She just couldn't find it.

Her solitude lasted three days. When he returned, he was even more abusive than before.

"Well, Maggie, did you enjoy your time alone while I was gone?" David asked.

"Actually, I did, David. You just weren't gone long enough. What happened? Nancy wouldn't sleep with you?"

"Hell no, it was a wasted trip from the beginning. All she did was stay on the phone with her girlfriend."

"What, you want me to tell you how sorry I am that it didn't go your way? Well, I'm not going to, David. You see, I just don't care anymore who you sleep with. All I know is that I want a divorce and you out of my house."

"No way am I giving you a divorce, and I'm not moving out of my house, Maggie. This belongs to me just like you do. You see, it's my money that has bought everything, and it's my money that pays the bills around here."

"No, it's not, David. I work six days a week, and my money goes into that account the same as yours. It's my money that pays for half of everything and all your trips. Do you think that it appears out of nowhere?"

"Maggie, I don't care where it comes from. I spent years in the military so that I could draw a check, so whatever I want, you just keep making sure that I have it, you clear on that?"

"Oh, I hear you loud and clear, David. Now you hear me. Give me a divorce."

"When hell freezes over, that's when I will give you a divorce, Maggie, not until. No judge will grant you one with me sick with cancer, and I can play it to the hilt. Now I'm going up to rest, and tomorrow morning, I am leaving for a few days. I'm going to go see a couple of friends."

"Fine! While you are gone, why don't you stay gone, like, forever, David?" Maggie screamed.

When he came home from his weekend trip, he was all smiles and strutting around like a chicken. Maggie asked him, "What's wrong with you?"

"I just had the most wonderful three days of my life. My dear friend Shawn and I, we enjoyed his wife together. It was fantastic. I didn't want to leave, but I had to come home to you."

"No, you didn't. You could have stayed. Better yet, why not move in with them?"

"Maggie, you really should take some lessons on how to make a man feel good," David said.

"Well, I like sex, David. I just don't like it with you and being humiliated. You sit in your room and watch all these porn movies, and you think you are this great porn star, like everything revolves around you."

"Well, deary, maybe you should try and watch them sometime. Believe me, you could learn a lot from them. Watching other people have sex is a real turn-on."

"Well, David, I guess you better go find someone who is into that sort of thing because you are not going to find it around here. And while we're on the subject, I want you to know that I will never ever have sex with you again."

"Maggie, Maggie, you are my wife, and if and when I want sex with you, you will give it to me one way or the other, darling."

"No, I won't, David. I'll cut your heart out before you touch me again."

"Ouch. Touchy, aren't we? Well, don't worry, I'm too exhausted right now anyway. I'm going to take a nap. Maybe later, dear."

It was Sunday, and Maggie had nowhere to go. The girls had things they were doing, so she called a friend to see if she wanted to go to the movies, but she was busy, so she sat downstairs with the TV on, watching the door all night.

Two months went by, and one Friday, he brought a woman home with him and told her she was going to stay for the weekend. Maggie had seen her before but couldn't place where, and then it dawned on her: it was at the last meeting the Legionnaire had held; that was where she had seen her. David introduced them, and Maggie said, "If you will excuse me, I have to go to work." And she left.

Later, they came to the bar and sat there talking. The woman tried to get Maggie in the conversation, but David told her, "Gail, leave her alone. She has to work."

Gail left on Monday, and when Maggie came home from work, David started in on her. "I don't have to tell you how you embarrassed me by not having anything to do with Gail."

She looked at him. "I embarrassed you? How do you think I felt, David? You brought a woman to my home and stayed with her. What's wrong with this picture?"

"All she wants is to be friends with you, Maggie. She's lonely and needs a friend."

"Sorry about her luck, but I'm not her friend."

"It's good that you're home early, Maggie. I needed to talk to you."

"What do you want now, David?"

"We are going to have a party at the legion for my peers. I am going to run for state office, and we have to show them that I can handle it. I want you to have it decorated in taste, and we are to have a sit-down meal. Don't look like I expect you to cook. I want it catered, and I want music. It will be dressy, so make sure that you wear black pants and a white shirt, okay?"

"What are you talking about? You just said it was dressy."

"Oh, I forgot. You and Paul are to work the bar, Maggie. My peers expect class at these functions, and, dear, that you are not. Gail will be with me at this function."

"I am not working the bar for you. You get someone else to do it."

"There is no one else, Maggie. You are it, and you will work it, if you want to keep your job, darling."

She worked that stupid party, and when she thought she couldn't take any more, here came David with a man. He introduced her as his wife. "This is Maggie. Maggie, I want you to meet Tony, a dear friend of mine." This Tony guy stood there and looked at her from head to waist as that was as far as he could see.

After a couple of minutes, she asked, "Well, do I pass inspection?"

"Sorry, you just remind me of someone I used to know," Tony said.

"Well, good for them. Now do you want anything to drink?"

"A beer would be nice, so how long have you and David been married?"

"Too long, I'd say. Why, what has he told you anyway?"

"Nothing really, just that he has found it harder to leave you lately."

She bust out laughing, so hard that David came over and told me to be quiet. "Maggie, you are embarrassing my peers."

"I don't care, David. If they don't want to hear me laugh, then they can go to the other room ."

"Maggie, Adam is here tonight, and you better be nice to him." Adam came in, sat down, and asked, "I would like to go to dinner with you one night."

She looked at him and, in a voice that left no arguments, said "no." She walked to the far end of the bar to where Paul was standing. "Maggie, what's wrong? Are you okay?"

"Yeah, I will be."

At the end of the evening, two of the guests walked up to Maggie and introduced themselves as April and Shawn. "Hello, what can I do for you?"

"We're friends of David's, and we thought that maybe you should know a few things. Do you ever get on Facebook?"

"No, why?" Maggie asked.

"Well, you need to." And they pulled out their phone and handed it to her. That was when she saw these pictures of David and another woman together. Every page was of them in each other's arm s, posing for pictures. It didn't matter that he was married because she was too. Perhaps they thought no one would see them, or maybe that was what they wanted.

"Why are you showing me these?"

Shawn spoke and said, "We like David and Brittany, but what he is doing just doesn't set well with us. Some of the other people at this club know what he is doing. They go to the meetings with him."

"I see, and who would that be?"

"One of them is Dave. He is running for the next commander here at the Club, and his wife, Alice, she is the president of the womens club. He is lying to you and to everyone else to get what he wants," April said.

"And how well do you know them ?"

"David spent a weekend with us, and we talked about everything."

"So you are the one that shares your wife with him, and I'm supposed to believe you?"

"Look, Maggie, we don't care whether you believe us or not. We just thought you should know," Shawn said.

Maggie didn't get to confront David after the party; he left with Gail and didn't come home. Mandy came over the next morning, wanting to go shopping. David still wasn't home when Maggie got back. She took her bags and went to her room . She never thought about shutting the door and locking it, and when she came out of the closet, there stood David. She could tell he had been drinking, and when she tried to go around him, he stopped me and said, "Why did you turn Adam down, Maggie? I made it clear to you that you were his woman, even though you are still my wife."

"No, David, I don't belong to Adam, and I don't belong to you. Yes, we are married and share a home, but we live separate lives."

"Well, Maggie, I guess we are going to have to consecrate our marriage again then, aren't we?"

"No, we don't. I won't have sex with you, David, so you just better get that idea right out of your drunk head."

David grabbed her and shoved her toward the bed. "You're my wife, sweetheart, and if I want to have sex with you, I will with your consent or not. It doesn't matter to me, my dear."

As he was walking toward her, unbuckling his belt, the doorbell rang, and Maggie ran toward the stairs and opened the door. She could hear him cursing upstairs. She opened the door, and there stood her darling daughter and grandchildren. She was never so pleased to see anyone in her life. "Amy, how good it is to see you, honey. Come in."

"Hi, Mom. I hope we're not interrupting you and Dad, but I was wondering if the kids could stay with you for a while."

"Of course, they can. And no, you are not interrupting anything. Why don't you just let them stay overnight? And I can bring them home tomorrow."

"Are you sure, Mom, that you don't mind?"

"Of course not. I haven't had them over in a while, and I really miss having them here."

David didn't say anything to Amy or the kids when he came downstairs, just went out the front door and left. Amy looked at me. "What's wrong with him?"

"The same old thing, honey. Don't worry about it. I don't. Besides, the kids and I are going to have a great time watching movies and eating popcorn all night." They squealed with delight and started jumping up and down, kissing their mom goodbye, and running to the basement to turn on the television set. She bid Amy goodbye, hugged her, and told her to be careful and that they would see her tomorrow. Amy waved goodbye and drove off.

The kids and Maggie settled in to watch movies, and she prayed that David wouldn't come in drunk. She asked them, "Okay, guys, what do you want to watch first?" And she put it on for them. She went upstairs so that she can make popcorn.

They were sitting on the couch when he came home. David went straight up to his room, where he stayed the rest of the night, and she thanked God for that. The kids fell asleep at around midnight. She covered them up and sat in a chair the rest of the night with them.

The next morning, they didn't want to go home, so they took off and went shopping for school. Maggie let them get what they wanted, which wasn't much, and then they went to lunch, and she took them home from there. She had to work that night and still had to go home and get her stuff.

No one was home when Maggie got there, so she ran in, grabbed everything, and left. Her solitude didn't last long. As soon as she unlocked the doors, David came strolling in with Adam before anyone else got there. David began, "Maggie, I'm going to tell you again that you belong to Adam . And as you are his property, he can touch you or do whatever he wants to, and that means having sex with him, if that's what he wants."

She looked at both of them and, in a calmvoice, said, "Well, I guess you both better go find someone else for your roles as a partner because this girl belongs to no one. And that means you, David, and also you, Adam . I will not, at any time, play your games. No one owns me. You both got that?"

"Damn you, Maggie. You will be his woman if I have to tie you to him."

"Get a life, David. You will never make me do something like that. I have never cheated on you, and I won't do it with your consent either, so forget it." They didn't get to say anything else because people started coming in, and Maggie just ignored them for the rest of the night.

Later that week, David came to her. "Honey, I need you to go to the bank and cash this check for me while I pack a bag. I'm leaving for the next three days, and I need cash. Make it for five hundred dollars. I'll use the card to pay for my room."

"No, you can cash it as you are leaving, David. You don't need me to do that for you."

"Fine, I'll do it myself. Sooner I leave, the better."

"You got that right."

When he came home, the first thing he said was "Maggie, go to the bank for me. I need eight hundred dollars."

"What do you need that kind of money for, David?"

"It doesn't matter. I need it, so unless you want to do my packing for me, then go to the bank." He left as soon as I got back, and he was gone for two days this time.

When he returned, he said, "I need two thousand dollars. I'm leaving for Texas, and I will be gone a week. I'm leaving first thing in the morning, so I need you to do the laundry when you get back."

"Do it yourself, David. I'm not your maid."

About that time, his hand came out and pushed Maggie up against the wall. "You just do what I tell you, Maggie, and you won't get hurt."

David had been gone for two days. Maggie had been asleep, and a sound or something woke her up. She sat straight up in the bed and listened; there it was again, a soft sound. She crept to the top of the stairs. She was breathing heavily not from fatigue but from fear—genuine fear. She stood there at the top step looking over the railing, knowing that someone was down there, and then the lights flickered off and stayed off. There it was, a man's shadow she saw from the moonlight coming through the window. It took her all of a second to put the pieces together, and the fear kicked in at an overwhelming rate. Her heart was pounding so loud in her ears that she knew that he could hear it.

Slowly, she started backing toward her room, praying that he hadn't seen her, and quietly shut the door and locked it. She twisted in the darkness and heard soft footfalls on the stairs. She went to the balcony door, unlocked it, and ran across it and down the back stairs, and she didn't stop till she got to her neighbor's house. She started pounding on the door. They opened it, and she all but pushed them back in and closed it. "I need to use your phone to call the police. There is someone in my house." They looked at her like she was crazy. She didn't care how crazy she sounded; it was the truth.

When the police got there, they walked her through everything that had happened and asked if she saw the person. "I only saw a shadow."

They told her, "Without seeing their face, we don't have much to go on. Do you want us to call someone to come stay with you, or do you have a friend that maybe you can go stay with?"

"No, I don't want to disturb anyone this late. I think I'll just go to a hotel for the night." She asked them to wait for her to change and if they would follow me there.

The next morning, Maggie called David and asked him where he was and if he had come home last night. "No, I'm still in Texas, where I have been for two days. Why, what has happened?"

"Someone was in the house last night, and the police were called but could not find anyone, and there was no broken windows or jammed doors."

"Maggie, are you okay? Did they hurt you?"

"No, I'm fine. It's just I thought it may have been you, David."

"Why would I do that to you, Maggie? Do you think so little of me?"

"Well, yes, I do. After all that you have done to me, David, what do you expect?"

Maggie was in the kitchen later that morning. When she heard the click of the lock, her heart went to her throat as she turned around and saw Pamela standing there. She grabbed the back of a chair, and Pamela came in, asking, "Are you okay, Maggie? What's wrong?"

"Nothing, you just scared me."

"Mag, why would I scare you like that? You knew I was coming over this morning."

"Oh, Pamela, I forgot. It's been hectic around here. Someone broke in on me last night. I guess I'm still shaky."

"Who broke in on you? Did you see them?"

"No, just a shadow, that's all. The police followed me to the hotel, and I stayed there the rest of the night."

"Maggie, was it David you saw?"

"Pamela, I don't know. All I do know is that it scared me almost to death."

"Do you want to come stay with me for a while till you can get it together?" Pamela asked.

"No, that's okay. I'll be fine. I went and bought some new door locks, and I'm fixing to put them on. Want to help me, sis?"

When David came home, he couldn't get into the house; and when he called, wanting to know why, Maggie told him that there were too many keys to the house, and she changed the locks. "I have your key. If you want to, come get it."

She was not expecting him to bring a woman with him. He walked up to the counter and said, "Maggie, this is Brittany. She is going to be staying the weekend at the house with me. Brittany, this is Maggie, my wife."

She came up to her and said, "Nice to meet you again. David has told me so much about you."

"Hello, it's nice to meet you, Brittany, I have seen you some somewhere. Weren't you at the first meeting that I went to for the auxiliary?"

"Yes, I didn't get to talk to you though. It was a busy weekend."

"Yes, it was."

Maggie pretty much ignored both of them while she was in her house. She didn't even know if she slept in his room; she just didn't care. And when she left on Sunday evening, David was as cruel as ever. "Why do you intentionally embarrass me by not talking to her while she was here?"

"David, why did you bring another woman into my house to stay with you? Are you openly telling me about your affair with her?"

"We are not having an affair, Maggie. She just needs a friend, and I thought you could be one for her. She's going through a rough period right now. She just found out her husband is cheating on her."

"Like you're not. I'm not stupid, David. If it's not her, then it's someone else." She had no idea that he had been seeing Brittany for two years until a friend of theirs asked if Maggie had been on Facebook lately. "Facebook again. No, I try not to go there to look at it. Why, is David on there again with his woman?"

"Maggie, you really need to get on there and look at what is being posted."

She had no clue what she was talking about until she opened the page, and out jumped David and Brittany posing for pictures with their arm s around each other at parties, with her saying, "This is my man," and him saying, "This is my beautiful woman." They posted pictures going into restaurants, hotels, elevators, and cars. They had pictures taken of everything they did together and every place that they stayed. It didn't seem to matter that he was a married man or that she was still married. Perhaps they thought no one would show them to her.

David started bringing her to the house every weekend, and Maggie would just leave and go to work. When she would leave, he would come to her, get in her face, and say, "Can't you be nice? She just wants to be friends with you for god's sake."

"Friends with me? What's wrong with this, David? We are still married, and you're bringing home your girlfriend to my house, where I live. Have you forgotten that?"

"How can I forget it, Maggie? I have to look at you every day that I'm here, and you make me

sick."

"Well, I can remedy that real quick. First thing in the morning, I'm filing for a divorce, and you won't have to look at me anymore, David," Maggie said.

"I will not give you a divorce. I will fight you till hell freezes over, Maggie. You will never get a divorce from me, and you will never get away from me alive, and that's all I have to say on the subject."

They were in the kitchen staring at each other across the counter.

"Oh, no, David, that's not all there is to it. You are married to me, but you don't own me," Maggie said.

"You are my property, and there is no one going to take you from me as long as I want to keep you!" David yelled. His face turned red, and he clenched his fist. His eyes were staring at her with such hate.

"You look at me like a stranger, instead of the fragile soul you made me. You look at me as the enemy. It's as if all our love became pain, and all the pain became hatred."

"All I feel for you is hatred Maggie, but you will stay married to me till you die."

"You are nothing more than a monster, you know that? And you just keep trying to make me weaker than you. You threaten me. You abuse me, yet you still want to keep me. I tell myself daily that I will never allow myself to go back to you, David. I tell myself it would be wrong, that you would continue to hurt me and try to keep me in your traps, wearing those awful chains you made for me. I was so confused but not now. Now I know better. I will never allow you to hurt me ever again. I will never go back to that kind of life again. I have made an arm or for my heart against you, and you will never drag me down that road again. You have caused me to realize that you are nothing but a joke."

She looked in the mirror, and all she saw was sadness; all the emotions had been pushed from her. Where there was once love and happiness was now just a hollowness. "I had more love for you than you could ever imagine, David. I was kind and gentle, but you never saw that. I invented every excuse for staying with you, and you... you gave me every reason to leave."

"Maggie, you're a piece of work. I'll give you credit for that. You know why I married you? It was because of your father. He made me marry you because I told him I was in love with Pamela. Yes, Pamela, your sister. I told him I had been in love with her from the moment I saw her. Believe me when I tell you, when I met you, I tried to love you and told myself that I was in love with you. But it was just pretend. I never could love you no matter how much I tried. But your father, he saw how I looked at her, and he told me that he would not allow me to have Pamela. He said I wasn't good enough for her. He kept telling me that I had asked you to marry me, that I had been living with you, and that I better keep my mouth shut and marry you, are walk away from everyone, and that included Pamela. He said that there was no way I would ever have her for my own, that she was his baby girl and deserved better than me. Don't look so shocked, Maggie. Even your own father knew you weren't worth keeping. He always put her first, just like I did. He loved her and not you."

"You're a liar, David. Everything you've said is a lie. My father wouldn't do that to me."

"He not only did do it but also said it, darling, and threatened to kill me if I so much as said a word to you or his beloved Pamela. But she already knew how I felt for her. I told her years ago. Yes, she knew. Don't you get it? No one wants you, no one wants to be around you, and no one loves you, Maggie not even your own father loved you."

David liked to be cruel, and his words hit their mark, and he knew it. Maggie hoped against hope that he would just walk away from her, but he wanted to fight with words and his fist. He kept slapping the counter with every vile word he said.

He had already done irreparable damage, so he might as well finish what he started, David thought.

As tears streamed down Maggie's face, he put his hand on her shoulder, leaned in close, and asked, "What's wrong? Did I say something wrong?"

She shoved his hand away. "Don't touch me, David." And all the words she had held back came tumbling from her mouth, words that she thought she would never say out loud. The instant they were out, she knew they had hit home and that nothing would ever be the same again. The gloves were off, and she wasn't going to run.

David's temper started to sizzle, and Maggie had no time to take cover or duck. He hit her harder than he ever had before, and she knew not to say another word, but she couldn't help it. She started to circle around the counter with blood oozing from her mouth, and tears streaming down her face and looked at him, and said, "You want to fight, David? Fine, I'm ready when you are. I'm not running from you anymore."

His temper went red hot, and he started slapping the counter even harder and advancing forward. Maggie had never gone this far into a fight with him before, but she wasn't backing down, not this time. She would fight him till one of them was down and not moving. When she reached the corner of the counter, she picked up her baseball bat and said, "I'm ready. Are you, David?" "Because hell is where you are going."

He looked at her, and his face turned crimson. His eyes popped wide open. He smiled and spat out words like a machine gun. Every word ories of him caused her to abruptly stop. She couldn't just leave him lying there hurt. She closed her eyes, took a deep breath, and steeled herself. You have to think of your future without him, Maggie. You are in command of your mind and your destiny. They lie in your hands, not his. She couldn't believe she had left him lying here.

Once on his feet, the room swayed, causing him to lose his balance, and he reached for the counter. His foot slipped, and he fell and hit his side on the corner of the counter, causing a scream to escape in pain. This meant that Maggie had really hit him and broken his ribs;

his memory was a little fuzzy. He called Adam to come take him to the hospital; he told him he had missed the damn step, yelling at Maggie. She had done a real job on him with that bat. I never saw it coming, David thought.

At the hospital, he ran his fingers through what little hair he had. They had to take xrays of his arm where she hit him, to make sure that it wasn't broken. He snarled at the nurse; he was in pain, and she wasn't helping pressing on his ribs as she wrapped them. Maggie had never done anything like that before. She always just took his abuse. He kept asking himself where she had gotten the guts to fight him. He knew one thing: he had to watch it for a while and get rid of that bat for sure. Her compulsion to fight with me tonight was strong. I'm going to have to break her of it and quick.

When Maggie went back home, the house was dark, so she opened the door and threw the lights on to make sure he wasn't waiting for her. As she went through the house, there was no sign of him. She took her bat and locked all the doors, including hers, and lay down on the bed; she didn't even take her clothes off in case he tried something.

David stayed with Adam that night; he didn't want to go home. Hell, she was probably waiting on him ; it would be just like her since he could barely move. Adam finally asked David, "So what really happened to you this afternoon?" I know you didn't fall down those stairs, you didn't have that much to drink this afternoon.

"Well, I guess I better tell you, just in case she comes at you, at least you'll have time to duck." David told him a few things; he didn't want to tell him all of it.

"You want me to talk to her for you?" Adam asked.

"She is not going to listen to you or anybody, Adam . She's mad. I'll just let her stew for a while."

When Adam got up the next morning he decided he was going to talk to Maggie, and he wasn't going to take her shit.

The doorbell rang. As Maggie came down the stairs, she looked out and saw Adam standing there. She yelled, "Just a minute!" Maggie opened the door. "What do you want?"

"I want to talk to you about, David," Adam said.

"What, you his errand boy now?"

"No. I want you to know I will not stand for you treating people like you did David."

Maggie narrowed her eyes at him as he continued to talk. "What did you say?"

"You heard me. Don't pretend you didn't," Adam snapped.

"Get out of my house now, Adam, and don't you ever tell me how to act."

A cruel sneer formed on his mouth; he leaned forward, eyes burning straight into hers. "There is no way that you took down David. Who did you have to help you?" Did you and Paul gang up on a helpless dying man, who is trying to take care of you? I don't understand how you could do something like that Maggie."

It was an effort to remain silent, her animosity toward him was showing, she tried to suppress her hatred for him, when he put is hand on her shoulder. Take your hands off me Adam ."

"Don't you ever touch me again or so help me you will look worse than David does.

"Maggie, I don't want to fight you. You will just get hurt."

Her anger was getting the better of her. She closed the distance between them, lowered her voice, and said, "You want to meet my backer, Adam ?"

Page of Love and Hate

About that time, David came walking in and told him to go home. "I'll see you in a little while." Fires of fury and hatred smoldered in his eyes; he was mad, but he saw the bat in my hand. David looked at her. "Let's get back to what we were talking about yesterday before you saw fit to attack me."

"I don't remember it that way, David. Correct me if I'm wrong, but you started the fight when you hit me and brought blood."

"Yes, but you provoked me, and you know damn well you did." It was an effort to remain silent; her animosity toward him was burning hot. "Maggie, as far as owning you, when we said 'I do,' you became mine. And yes, I own you, and I will till the day you die. And just so you know, when you die, believe me, I'll be there at your funeral just so I can stand at your grave and piss on it. That's what I think of you. Oh, one more thing, don't even think of going to an attorney, Maggie, because if you do, believe me, not even Adam will want you then," David said.

"You go straight to hell, David, because that's where you belong. You are nothing but pure evil, and I hate you from the depths of my soul. You may think you have won, but you haven't. I will get away from you and make you pay for all the pain and misery you have inflicted on me."

"I haven't even begun to inflict pain on you, Maggie. When I do, you will know it." And he turned to walk out the door.

She had to ask, "David, when you said you loved me, I took you at your word. You said that I would be your soul mate forever. Then one night you told me you were in love with my sister and not me. Why did you stay with me all these years? You should have left me. It would have been kinder. Now I must not show bitterness to my own family because of you. If it wouldn't hurt them so bad, I'd see you six feet under and never shed a tear. There's so much hatred that I never knew I could hate that much."

David turned and stared at her. "Maggie, don't push me. I've given you fair warning."

"I see the person you are, I know the person you are, you are the person that hurt me."

"I gave you freely my love, yet you tried dominance, you tried manipulation and hurtful words. All I ever wanted was to love you, I gave you my soul and yet you wanted more."

"You know, as painful as it is tolerating my heartbreak, it's still better than tolerating all your lies and cheating. Just remember, David, the past, it can't be changed, deleted, edited, or even forgotten. Life is short, and people don't forget."

"I don't regret my past, Maggie. I just regret the time that I wasted on you." And he turned and walked out the door. God, it felt so good to tell her how he felt. He no longer had to hide his feelings from her. But there is no way I will give her a divorce. I want her to suffer. I want her to hurt so bad that she will be begging me to kill her just to get her out of her misery.

Maggie thought of new beginnings- with her memories of him in thick ice." She thought of her future she would mould and build, her destiny, a destiny that lay in her hands."

His new life with Brittany left no room for her, not that he wanted her. He just wanted to keep her tied to him till the time was right to be rid of her for good. He had to try to suppress his hate that he felt for her in front of the kids and his friends, which shouldn't be hard. He was good at lying. At first, he felt guilty about cheating and lying to her, but that gave way to realizing how much he hated her. God, he would love to put his fist in her face and enjoy every punch. Now that would give him delight, a buzz he couldn't get from a bottle.

Maggie sat down on the couch and started to cry. She cried for all the years of abuse and lies she had put up with. Her whole life was nothing but a lie; all she had ever wanted was someone to love and to be loved back. She had wanted happiness and a home, and she had neither. She kept asking herself why Pamela had never said anything to her. Had she felt the same way about him all those years ago?

She told herself he had lied about her dad saying and doing those things. Then the memories were like yesterday, and as she remembered, all the little signs that she had pushed away came back to haunt her. Maggie knew, without a doubt, that he was telling her the truth about her dad. Her father had made a monster marry her, and her sister wouldn't tell her the truth. She thought about all the opportunities that Pamela had, had to tell her that he was in love with her. Pamela had kept quiet; was it because she loved him or didn't want to hurt her?

As she tried to get her head together, Maggie thought, My deepest fear is not that I'm inadequate but that he may be more powerful than I am. It's not the darkness that frightens me. It's David because I know what he is capable of.

David strode briskly down the sidewalk, his hair blown by the wind. He watched the clouds that had sprung up during the afternoon; he knew he was going to get wet before he got to his destination. He had to talk to Adam, and he had to help him with this problem he left at home. Brittany was going to be gone for the next two weeks, and he had to fix this problem before she returned. She wanted to get married, even though she knew he was not going to divorce Maggie, but she was pushing him to end things. Brittany knows I'm not going to give Maggie half of everything, including my pensions. I've worked too hard to get where I am to lose it to her.

Adam was waiting on him when he entered the restaurant. They put their heads together and tried to come up with some kind of idea that people, especially the girls, would believe. Adam came up with Maggie having an affair and him catching her at it. He said, "Then you could file against her, and the judge would believe you over her. Man, she is the one that has been working at a bar and leaving you alone every day. She knew you were sick and needed someone to watch over you. Hell, all the guys at the club would back you on this— well, all but one. And he has this thing for Maggie. That's good because we could use this poor sap of guy to our advantage."

The only thing that was the holdup was Adam, he wanted to have sex with her. Why? David didn't know. He wanted him to find a time to let him in the house. "I know, David, if I could be alone with her for an hour, she would come around, and I wouldn't have to force her."

"You think you are that good, Adam, that she will just fall into your arm s?"

"Hey, don't knock it. I have been known to sweep quite a few women off their feet."

"Yeah you probably did but they weren't Maggie either."

How was David going to let him in the house without her knowing— that was the hard part. He could just give him his key to let himself in with. That may be the answer but she would know where he got the key from. "I could crush some of my sleeping pills and put them in her drink. Yeah, I can do that. She will never know, but she keeps her doors locked all the time when she is at home. Oh well, I'll figure something out."

Pamela called Maggie to find out if she was okay and see what she was doing. "I'm fine. No, I'm not. I'm scared. In fact, I've been scared of everything. I'm afraid to close my eyes. I'm sharing a life with someone that's dishonest, someone that hates me, who doesn't care if I'm alive or dead. And I'm scared of being vulnerable to someone that want let me go, that keeps threatening me. I know I need to get away from him, but he has me watched and followed every day. The only place I feel safe is at work, Pamela. I just don't want to end up dead and him getting away with it. Do you understand what I'm saying? He will kill me the first chance he gets, and I'm not going to give him the chance," Maggie said.

"Maggie, you can go to the police and have an EPO put on him," Pamela said.

"And what good would that do? A piece of paper won't stop him in his tracks, and you know that. It would just make him even more determined. No, I'm going to do it my way, and maybe I will live another day. Pamela, I need to talk to you. David told me some things yesterday, and I need truthful answers from you. I want the whole truth when I see you this weekend."

Later that day, David came to the Legionnaire Club and sat with some of the guys. They were laughing at something he said. One guy asked him, "What happened to you?"

"I missed a step at home and fell down the stairs."

They laughed at him. "Man, don't you know those stairs are a death trap when you're drunk?" He laughed with them, and then he got up and told them he was leaving and that he would see them the next day.

About the time he started out the door, Adam came walking in. He shook David's hand as he left and said, "Later, bro." Adam went to the end of the bar and sat down next to Paul, asking what he was up to and how long he was staying.

Paul said, "As long as I want. You got a problem with it?"

"No, no problem . I just need to talk to Maggie after all you guys leave for the night," Adam said.

"Well, Adam, that's entirely up to her whether I leave or not and if she wants to be alone with you. Maggie, do you want me to leave with the rest of the guys so you can be alone with Adam ?"

"No, Paul, I don't want you to leave me alone with him. If anyone leaves, it should be him."

Adam jumped up, grabbed his phone, and called someone. They didn't hear a name, just him ranting about Paul and saying he would try the next day, and he left.

"Thank you for staying. If you don't mind, would you stay till I close tonight and go out with me, please?"

"Maggie, you don't have to ask. I wouldn't leave you to the likes of those two. How can you stay married to him anyway?" Paul wanted to know.

"Because he has threatened to kill me if I leave him. We live in separate parts of the house, Paul. We have not been husband and wife for four years, and he refuses to give me a divorce. He keeps telling me no judge will grant me one with him sick. And to tell you the truth, I think he lied about having cancer."

"Do you want a divorce, Maggie? 'Cause if you do, I know an attorney who will take your case. You will have to be truthful with her and tell her everything that has happened over the years. Don't think that I haven't seen the bruises and marks on you, and you try to hide them. We see them, Maggie, and some of us here don't like what he's doing to you. You know I like you, Maggie, and I don't want you getting hurt," Paul said. "I would love to spend time with you and take you out sometime. I think you need someone that you can talk to and someone that will be there if you need them. So want to go get something to eat when you close in ten minutes?"

"Yes, I would, if you are sure you don't mind being seen with me."

"I would love to be seen with you. You are a very beautiful woman. Any man would love to be with you— well, some men, I should say," he replied.

When she got home, David was gone, and she went to her room and locked all the doors. A little while later, she heard him come in and go to his room . The next morning, she was drinking a cup of coffee when he came into the kitchen. "Maggie, I'm leaving this afternoon for a couple of days. I'll be back this weekend, and thanks for asking how my ribs are."

She never said a word to him, just looked at him and walked off. She was outside when he left. She went back in to lock all the doors before she took a bath. She was going to meet Paul before she opened the bar. He had all the information for her about his attorney, and he didn't want anyone to know about it.

When Maggie got to work, Paul was waiting on her, so they went in together. He was talking. As she got everything ready to open up, he called out for her to come and look what he found. He was on Facebook, and what they saw was beyond words: there was David and Brittany smiling up at each other; he had his arm s wrapped around her. The more he scrolled, the madder she became. There were more pictures posted of themselves. There were pictures at the pool, at a bar, at the hotels they stayed in. But the one that got her attention was of her in a long white gown and him in a tuxedo with the caption that read "The new Mr. and Mrs. Jackson." She asked Paul to save all the pictures but send her that one, just in case they removed them from view.

"What are you going to do, Maggie?" Paul asked.

"I intend to get a divorce as soon as possible. I'll be calling the attorney Monday morning to start the process."

Paul and Maggie spent the weekend together going to the movies, riding the motorcycle and and going out to eat. He was a really nice guy, and she liked him.

When David came home on Sunday night, he never said a word about the pictures on Facebook, and she didn't ask. Maggie called the attorney on Monday and was told that the first available appointment she had open was a week from then. She said that would be fine. She wrote down the time to meet her and prayed she would still be alive. It was so bad at home that her children wouldn't come over to see her because he was there. They called three, sometimes four, times a day, but it wasn't the same as seeing them.

David and Maggie rarely spoke to each other, even though they lived in the same house. The hate she felt for him was consuming her, and she would pray that he would die a horrible death. She couldn't stand looking at him, and so she just stayed away.

David left again on one of his trips, and later that evening, Maggie was about to leave when there was a knock at the front door. David was in his hotel room, his head resting in his hands. He imagined his fingers curled tightly around her neck. He could actually feel it snapping in his mind, the feel of his fist smashing her face. His knuckles were white from clenching them. Pamela knocked again, yelling, "Maggie, you home?"

Maggie went to the door, and Pamela walked in. "I couldn't wait till next week to talk to you," Pamela said. "So what did the piece of dirt have to say to you?"

"Want to come sit down first?" Maggie asked.

"Do you have any caffeine in a bottle? Coke or Diet will do."

"Sure."

Pamela sat down and looked at Maggie. "Well, what happened?"

"Pamela, how long have you known that David was in love with you? Did he tell you before we married, and why in the hell didn't you tell me? You and Dad both let me marry a monster. Why?"

"Maggie, I'm so sorry. I knew you were in love with him, and he kept coming on to me. He cornered me one day and tried to kiss me, and I slapped him, told him to keep his hands to himself. He just said, 'Oh come on, you know I love you, Pamela. I have from the moment I saw you.' I told him to get the hell out of my house, that if he said anything to me again, I would tell Dad. I didn't know he had talked to Dad until after you married him," Pamela said.

"That still doesn't explain why you didn't come to me in the first place. You and Dad let me live in torture for not telling me the truth. Did you both think I was too feeble to know?" Maggie asked. "You have no idea what I've been through to keep my family from knowing the truth about him."

"Maggie, all I can say is I'm sorry, truly sorry. When he didn't say anything, I just assumed he still loved you. I told him there was no chance for him with me," Pamela said.

"As painful as it would have been to have my heart broken, it would have been better than being broken into tiny bits all these years."

"Sis, please don't hate me for not telling you. I couldn't hurt you by telling you."

Maggie looked at her and said, "I don't hate you, sis. I'm hurt that you never said a word all this time."

"Maggie, I sure hope that you don't. I love you, and I couldn't stand it if you did." Pamela began to cry. "I'm sorry."

Maggie put her arm around her and said, "Sh, don't cry. It's okay, you are my sister, and I love you too, and I could never hate you. Pamela, you want to stay here tonight so we can talk more?"

"Yeah, I would love to. But first things first, let's go get something to eat. I'm starved."

Maggie realized suddenly that she was hungry for the first time in days. They both started laughing and went out the door.

David came home early to try to catch her off guard; he wasn't expecting her to have company, especially Pamela. Maggie asked him, "What are you doing home? I thought you had a meeting."

"It was called off," he replied.

Two weeks went by with no problems from David or Adam . I know deep down that something is wrong. I just can't put my finger on it, Maggie thought.

Brittany had returned from her trip and she wanted to know if he had told Maggie that he was divorcing her. He told her no, but he would tell her when he returned home. David if you don't tell her I will leave you, I want be the other woman in your life. Brittany darling I love you and I intend to end things with her next week, so please stop threating to leave me. The next week, David announced, "I'm leaving for a week. I'll be in meetings, so don't call me if anything happens."

Later that day, he came to the Club and told the guys that he was leaving and to keep an eye on her. That, in itself, was strange because he never said things like that. What was he up to? I need to be careful, Maggie thought. She didn't want to go home that night, so she called a friend to see if she could stay there.

The next morning, she went home expecting to see him, but no one was there. But she hurried and did things so she could leave. After the third day, she felt it was safe to stay at home. She had closed the bar early, and was getting ready for bed when there was a knock on the door. Maggie wondered who it could be this late and started toward the door. Before she could get there, she saw the handle turn, and she was startled as the door opened, and he walked in. "What are you doing here, David? You're supposed to be on a trip," she stated.

"I don't plan on being here long, Maggie," David said.

David's fist hit her so hard that she fell from the force of it; she hadn't expected it, and she was stunned for a moment. He always did like to argue with hurtful words and his fist. He started shouting all these words of hatred to her— how much he despised her and how he loathed the ground she walked on. She was trying to get up off the floor when his fingers curled in her hair and he started pulling her up the stairs, and every bump on the stairs was making a bruise. Maggie was trying not to hit the stairs, but he was pulling her hair out.

He was still cursing her all the way to her room, where he flung her down on the floor. She started to get up, and his foot connected with her ribs and knocked the breath out of her. She heard something crack and knew he broke a couple of ribs. "That's for hitting me with that damn bat and breaking my ribs. How does it feel?" And he kicked her again.

She got on her knees, crawled up the side of the bed, and took a swing at him but missed. He just laughed at her, and he kicked her legs out from under her and kicked her again. She fell again, and with the pain, she can barely breathe. He grabbed her and threw her on the bed. David grabbed her with one hand and ripped her shirt off. She got a second breath and started kicking him, aiming for his chest. Maggie tried to roll off the bed; it hurt to move, but she knew she had to keep fighting him.

While laughing at her menacingly, he grabbed her again, held her in place, unbuckled her pants, and got them off her. David bent down and bit one breast and then the other, grabbing her between the legs and pinching her. She didn't know how he managed to get his pants down, but he did. He whispered, "This is for Adam, Maggie." When he entered her, Maggie thought she would die; he did everything he could to hurt her. He just continued to bite her all over her chest and stomach and pinching her while laughing.

He let go of her for a second, and she tried to get away from him, kicking and swinging her fist. He grabbed hold of her arm, twisted her over to her stomach, and entered her from behind. She started screaming from the pain, and he just grabbed her around the hips and shoved even harder. She couldn't breathe; the pain was something she could never have imagined.

When she thought he was done, he pushed her up on the bed and told her to open her mouth.

When she refused, he took hold of her hair again and slammed her head into the headboard, demanding that she open her mouth. She still wouldn't do as he demanded and clamped her mouth shut so tight that she could taste blood. His face lit up at once, knowing that he had power over her. When she still wouldn't open her mouth, he became angry; his face turned red because she refused to obey him and give in to him. He slammed her head again into the headboard, making her moan. He wanted to dominate her, but she kept fighting him.

"You made a terrible mistake, Maggie, by not taking Adam . Now you will pay the price," David said.

Every word he said, every violation of her body he made, only fueled the fire burning inside of her. "I will see you in hell, David." And she brought her knee up. She caught him by surprise and tried to twist away from him.

He grabbed her with both hands and bashed her head again, cracking the headboard, this time bringing blood from the side of her head. He looked at her and when he let go, she fell over. He knew, by looking at her and the blood, that he had killed her. He bent over to see if she was breathing; she wasn't, and he couldn't find a pulse. David snorted and said, "It's better you're dead anyway. Now I don't have to fight you in court." He got up and got dressed. He took another look at her and spat on her.

Then he thought, I need to leave in case someone heard her screaming and called the police. I'll come back later like I was just getting home. Everyone knows that I left. Yeah, that was what he would do. No one saw him enter, and his car was on the other street. He went out the back door to his car and left. He thought about calling Adam but decided not to. I need to stay away for a few hours in case someone did call the police when she started screaming.

When Maggie came to, she was by herself. She didn't know how long she had been out, and when she touched her head, her hand came back covered in blood. Slowly, she crawled from the bed and tried to walk to the bathroom . She hurt so badly, and it was hard for her to take a deep breath. She knew she had to clean herself up and get out before he came back and found her alive.

David started to think of what he had just done, but the damage was already done, and there was no going back now; he had killed her. And now he had to make it look like an accident. No one knew he was home. The girls thought he would be gone for a few more days. He can do this. All he had to do was keep his cool and go home. And when I get there, I'll pick her up and roll her down the stairs. That's all there is to it. If anyone asks how she had gotten all the bite marks, I'll just say, "Probably from her boyfriend. She has been cheating on me for years." Then I will be free from the past, David thought. I can finally start a new life with Brittany and live the life I want and was meant to have, not one that is expected of me.

Maggie crawled into the shower and turned on the hot water; it stung every part of her body, but she endured it. She got dressed and slowly made her way down the stairs and to the garage. She had just backed out and was going around the curve in the opposite direction when she saw headlights turn into the driveway. She knew it was David, and it scared her. As much as it hurt to move, she floored it to get somewhere safe, anywhere besides here. So she just drove and called a friend, knowing that if David saw her, he could catch her. Thankfully, she made it out of the subdivision and went to stay at her friend's house. She put her car in her garage so as not to be seen.

Kimberly opened the side door. When Maggie crawled out, Kimberly took one look at her and said, "Oh god, Maggie, you need to go to the hospital." She could hardly walk, and she was holding her side. "You need to get taken care of. You may have some broken ribs. What did he do to you?"

"Kimberly, you don't want to know. But it's okay, I'll heal. But you're right, I think my ribs are broken. But when he finds me gone, the hospital will be the first place he looks. I can't take a chance on him finding me there."

"Maggie, can you make it to my car? I'm taking you to the hospital." When Maggie held up her hand, Kimberly said, "Not around here. You're right, he will look there."

So she drove her to a hospital three counties away. They asked what happened, and Maggie said, "I fell down a flight of stairs." They didn't believe her and called the police. But she kept telling them the same thing. The Doctor wanted her to stay over night for observations but she refused, so they wrapped her broken ribs and gave her some pain medicine, and she left.

The next morning, Maggie called the girls to check on them. They were hysterical. "God, Mom, what happened? Dad called us early this morning and said he came home early and found blood all over the bed, the floor, and stairs. He said he couldn't find you anywhere. Are you okay? Where are you?" Mandy asked.

"I'm fine, honey, or I will be after a while. Right now, I'm at a friend's house... No, don't ask. I can't tell you. Just believe that I will tell you when I see you, and don't tell your father that you spoke to me, okay? Promise me, Mandy."

"Mom, he said some terrible things about you. He said that you have been cheating on him. He said it's been going on for years. He also said he begged you not to do that to him. He swore he loved you and would do anything to get you back."

"Honey, he is nothing but a liar. I have never cheated on him in all the years we have been married. That's just his excuse to get away with everything he has done. Mandy, do you believe what your dad said?"

"I don't know. No, Mom, I don't. I know you wouldn't do that. I know something has been wrong lately, and he stays gone all the time."

"Mandy, I have never lied to you or your sisters. I kept some things from you girls because of shame, but I would never lie to you. Honey, I need you to call your sisters and tell them the same thing I just told you, and make sure they don't tell your father anything. I will be in touch in a few days. Just know that I love you, and I'm okay, and I will tell you everything then."

When David pulled into the driveway, he thought he saw the garage door close the rest of the way, but that was impossible. She was upstairs dead. *Just my imagination.* When he went upstairs, he saw blood on the stairs, and he ran the rest of the way two steps at a time. Where the hell is she? I know she was dead. Think, David. Did you check her pulse to make sure? Yes, yes, I did. I know she wasn't breathing. Calmdown, she officially wasn't dead. You just didn't check close enough. Damn, where did she go? I have to find her quick before she goes to the police.

He called their children to see if she was with one of them and went about setting the scene: he didn't know what had happened, and he was worried for her safety. Now all he had to do was wait; everything was in motion.

Maggie called Mandy three days later and said, "You are the eldest, so I will start with you. I am going to file for a divorce first thing tomorrow. I need to be away from your father. Mandy, you will hear more lies he will tell, and none of them are the truth, and you will have to decide for yourself who is lying. But for now, that's all I can tell you. In a matter of days, everything will be out in the open." She called each of her children and told them the same thing. There were a lot of questions, and she wouldn't answer them. She asked them to wait a few days.

The next day, she went to see her attorney. When she saw Maggie, she just looked at her and said, "Where is he, Maggie? What did he do to you? You want me to send him to prison for the rest of his sorry life? I can do that right now. Just tell me where he is, and I'll have him picked up within the hour."

"No, Gail, I can't do that to my children's father, even though that's where he needs to be. I can't be that cruel."

"Maggie, you need to be strong and send him away for life. No man has the right to treat a woman like this," Gail told her.

"I know what I'm doing, Gail, and I promise he won't get the chance to ever hurt me again, not physically anyway."

Maggie took a police officer with her when she went home. She knew he would be there. When they walked in, he became this pitiful excuse for a man. He came up to her and said, "Honey, where have you been, and what happened? I came home early to find this awful mess in your room and on the stairs. I have been so worried."

The police officer stepped between her and David. "Sir, you need to back away from her. You need to go upstairs and pack a suitcase. You are not allowed to stay in the same house with her."

David started screaming, "This is my damn house, and I'm not leaving!" She is my wife and I will stay here with her."

The officer quietly asked him again to pack. "Sir, if you don't go pack, I will escort you out without your clothes."

"You can't make me leave my own home for no reason."

"I not only can remove you from your home but I also can arrest you and put you in jail."

David mumbled all the way upstairs, packed a bag, got in Maggie's face, and said, "This is not over, Maggie."

The police officer took him by the arm and said, "Mister, did you just threaten her?"

David stopped short and realized what he had said. He turned around and said, "No, I didn't. I just meant that it was my house and she could not have me leave like this."

"Mr. Jackson, yes, she can. We don't know what happened here. She hasn't said, but believe me when I say this: we will be watching you. And if you come anywhere near her at home or at her place of work, you will be arrested and confined in jail. Do you understand what I'm telling you?" the officer asked him.

"Yes, I understand completely, Mr. Officer, sir."

David stayed away from the house and her work, and two months went by without a word from him. Maggie slowly healed, and during this time, she had written six letters and given them to her attorney. There was one for each of the girls, her attorney, the police, and David, only to be given to them at her death.

David came to see Maggie and asked if he could please move back into the house because he couldn't afford to keep staying at the hotel. She looked at him. "You know, David, it's hard for me to remember my life before you. I can't seem to even make the comparisons anymore because all my memories have been replaced with you. They have the depth of a photograph that never leaves my mind. And as far you moving back in, if that's what you want, but you need to understand something now, David. I have filed for a divorce.

"And before you start screaming and threatening me again, there is something you should know. My attorney has letters that I wrote that plainly state that if I die an untimely or ill-given death, they are to arrest you. I have told them everything that you have done to me, going all the way back to the beginning, David.

I have told them about the verbal, mental and physical abuse. I have told them everything even about the rapes. I know the statue for rape is past but everyone including your children will know what you did and continued to do. Your so called friends will know that you are nothing but a liar, cheat and an abuser, I even told them about all the times you tried to kill me David." I have hidden all this from our children and friends and you left me no choice but to tell them everything.

Maggie you better not have mentioned a thing about our past, what happened was between you and me, but if you did I promise you I will kill you." I will get away with it to, you know that the miltary said I have P.T.S.D. they want do a thing to me, but you will be dead."

David do you think I'm stupid I have everything on tape including your threat you just made to kill me."

"You bitch I should have killed you years ago,"David snapped.

I left the children a letter, telling them what kind of father they have, and it will be up to them if they want anything to do with you. I also told them about Brittany and how long the two of you have been seeing each other. Now if you want to stay here until the divorce is final, then stay. Just remember that you are still being watched and will continue to be watched until I decide to stop it," Maggie replied.

"Fine. I can't live like this anymore. I can't stand to be around you for much longer. I need the love and attention from Brittany. She loves me, and I love her with all my heart. She makes waking up in the morning worthwhile."

"Then why don't you go stay with her?"

"You know damn well her divorce isn't final. I'll sign your damn divorce papers, Maggie, and I'll even use your attorney so things go smoother just to be rid of you."

"That works for me, David. I'll make the appointment now. And I'll definitely be glad to be rid of you. There are times when I doubt everything. There are times that I regret everything. You have taken everything from me, David. Yet I gave you everything and wasted all the time I've spent on us. You found so much pleasure in hurting and hating me that you couldn't see what was right in front of you. You cheated on me. You lied to me. To you, it was all just a game. You are someone who is a liar, or is that too harsh a word for you? You are the person who would get caught and say, 'Oops, I'm sorry.' This isn't about you finding yourself another woman. These were lives you messed with. You are so much worse than a cheater. You killed something beautiful, and you killed it while its back was turned."

David just looked at her and said, "Thank you for letting me move back to my home. You know, Maggie, that was a pretty good speech. I'll have to try and remember it."

Two days later, they both went in to talk to Gail. "I want the house, the checking account, my car, and almost all the contents in the house." He went on to tell her that he would not pay Maggie alimony and that she could not file for anything pertaining to his pension or his retirement. He said that, once the divorce was final, she lost all interest in his allotments as they were from the military.

Gail looked at him and said, "Mr. Jackson, no judge is going to grant you everything. It is my understanding that Maggie has bought all the furniture and the decorations for that house. You have not worked and have not helped her in any way, isn't that so?"

"No, I haven't worked, but it was my money that bought everything. It was my pensions that went into the checking account that she used," David snapped.

"Now, Mr. Jackson, you know that she has been the one working, and her money goes into that account the same as yours. It is stated that you are the one that has been taking money out of that account for your trips and your lover, isn't that so?" Gail asked him.

"What? Is this some kind of witch hunt? I thought we were here to sign papers for a divorce?" David yelled.

"Mr. Jackson, I'm asking the same questions the judge will ask you, if this goes before him. Do you really want all your dirty laundry aired in public? Think very hard before you answer that because I will reveal every sordid detail to the judge, and you may go to prison for attempted murder. Do you want to chance it?"

"No. What do you want, Maggie?"

"I want a lot of things, David. I want a life where I'm not afraid to close my eyes. I want a life where I don't have to be afraid of being raped and abused mentally and physically. I want someone who doesn't get off hurting me for the pleasure of it, but mostly, I want to be away from you. I want my life back and to be able to find true love, not lies. I want the house sold. You can live there till then, and you are to keep it up and pay the mortgage on it. And don't be late, not once, or I will have you in court," Maggie said.

"Well, why not just take everything, Maggie?"

"I don't want everything, David. I'm willing to split all of it. Take whatever you want from the house, but you will not touch the checking account. However, I will pay you a thousand dollars a month for a year and a half. That's all you are worth. And don't come begging me to give you more when you find you can't make it alone. David, just sign the papers and drop the drama. No one cares anymore." Not once did he tell them that Maggie was eligible for half his pensions, and she didn't think of it at the time. She just wanted it over and to be away from him.

By the end of the month, Brittany had moved into the house, both of them acting like they had always been together. They acted as though Maggie had never been married to David and nothing had ever happened between her and him. It wasn't until a friend of his came to Maggie and asked if she had gotten half of his benefits. She said, "No, I wasn't entitled to them until he died."

He cocked his head. "Who told you that? Dear, you are entitled to half of everything. You go back to your attorney and have them refile. You hear me?"

Maggie asked Gail to check into it for her, and when she contacted the military, they told her that since he had that clause put into the divorce, Maggie couldn't touch anything unless he withdrew it. "I'm sorry, Maggie. I let you down and let him get one over on us, and I'm so sorry."

Gail had her call David and ask him to sign a letter stating that she could draw on his pensions. "No way. I need every penny to take care of Brittany and myself. It's the first time I feel like a real man. Besides, I need to make her feel special. I love this woman, and I intend to make sure she has everything she ever wants. You will never draw off me, Maggie. I am going to make sure of that."

David saw their children and told them that, as soon as his divorce was final, he was getting married. "I know you think that it's awful because your mother and I are still legally married. But Brittany and I have been seeing each other for five years. You may not like it, but in time, I know you will come to love her as much as I do." All three girls tried to distance themselves from David and Brittany, even though she went out of her way to make them feel wanted and loved.

David did everything to try to make Maggie's life miserable. They would come to her workplace and sit there, and he would cuddle and kiss her and tell people how much they loved each other. When no one was around, especially Brittany, he would make little snide remarks. "David, why don't you just leave? I don't care what you do or who you do it with. Just leave me alone and let me have a life."

"Maggie, you are never going to have a life, just like you are nothing to me. You never have been, and I am so glad to be rid of you. I finally have a beautiful woman who loves me and makes me happy. That's something that you never did. Oh, it's not that you didn't try, Maggie. You did, but really, who could love something like you? Nobody wants you, and nobody will ever love you. Why can't you understand that? I mean, just look at you," David said cruelly.

"David, who are you trying to convince, me or yourself, that I'm not capable of finding love? Whichever it is, I don't care. I will never allow you to hurt me again, not with words or physical pain, ever again. As for you being rid of me, that goes two ways, David. The only difference is that I loved you and never lied about it, and I can say that with a clear conscience. And the only reason you stayed with me is that no one else would have you. The only reason Brittany wants you is for whatever money you spend on her. You have spent more money on her in one year than you ever did on me and the children in the thirty years we were married. To me, you are nothing but a liar, a user, and a cheat, and I hope that you burn in hell for all the things that you did to me."

"Well, if that's how you feel, I'm glad we are no longer together. At least I have a special woman who loves me deeply, and I can say without a doubt that I love her. That's more than I could ever say about you, Maggie."

"Gee, David, you always did know what to say to hurt people, but you can't hurt me anymore. I hope you find what you are looking for, because you can't buy love and that's what you keep trying to do."

"I say what I feel, and I feel nothing for you. I never have. Oh, I tried to tell myself that I was totally in love with you. I guess I fooled everybody, including myself."

Two months after the divorce was final, Brittany and David were married. They lived in Maggie's house, acting like David built it for her. They acted like they were great friends, something Maggie can't be with David. As she got to know Brittany, she found her nice, nothing like she had expected. Even though she knew David was married when she started an affair with him, Maggie did find out that it was him lying to them both to get what he wanted.

David and Brittany lived in Maggie's house for four years before it sold; he wouldn't sell it. Whenever there was an offer on it, he would turn it down. Maggie finally told him to sell the house, or she would take him back to court. The house sold three weeks later. She found out then that he had refinanced it to the max so she wouldn't receive anything from the sale after the mortgage was paid off.

She wished them well, and she hoped David would get everything he deserved. She hoped that everything that he ever did to her would come back to haunt him. She wanted him to remember her and know that everybody knew him for who and what he was. She tried to shield her children from all the hurt and pain that their father dished out every day to her. And she was sorry that they had to find out what he was capable of. She had told them that he loved them and that he would never have hurt them, that he just had a problem with her. She encouraged the girls to spend time with him not only for their sake but also for their children's; they needed to know that he loved them. He tried to spend a lot of time with the grandchildren; he loved them, and she didn't want them to abandon him like he did his family. When you get right down to it, family is all you have; and without them, you are left alone.

Maggie smiled all the time so that nobody knew how broken and lonely she really was. The worst kind of pain is when you are smiling to stop the tears. When you wake up one morning and realize that you are not afraid to live again. That the greatest thing in life is happiness and someone to love, and something to hope for."

At work, life had gone down the tube. David had been elected to the State Officers position, and Dave, became the new commander. Dave and his wife, Alice, tried everything to have her fired. So far, the board of directors wouldn't have any of it. Since the time that he took office, Maggie had been harassed every day. He, Adam, and Jack continuously found reasons to confront her together when no one was around. On one occassion Jack stood at the end of the bar and got in my face and screamed at the top of his lungs at me." the only thing that I had said was it's her birthday Jack.". Paul had stood up for her a few times when they came in to harass her; he just happened to be there to hear them. She knew David was behind a lot of it, but it was mostly Alice who wanted her gone for some reason she just didn't like Maggie.

Alice would tell me things about Paul and say that he just wanted a sugar mom my to take care of him. I'm not sure why she did this maybe she thought I was taking Paul away from them or her. They had all been friends in the past, and now Paul was spending his time with Maggie.

Maggie still tried to be nice to all who came into the Legionnaire but there were some who would think you weren't nice enough to them no matter what you did. Maggie went out of her way to be nice to Alice and Dave. I don't know why they dislike me so much." But I can't change the way people think or act, all I know is I'm tired of trying to be nice to people like that. They may be people out there who don't like me, but they don't even know me. There are people who do like me because they took the time to know me for who I am.

It has been two years now, and Maggie has been dating the same guy, even though it was hard for her to trust. She thought she had learned a lot from her past, and she would never let anyone hurt her again like David did. Paul had helped her understand that she needed to see a therapist for emotional, psychological, and assault problems to get over everything that David had done. It was the best advice he had given her.

Maggie no longer worked at the legionnaire. She had been harassed too much to even enjoy working there. When she goes there with Paul, she is ignored by the commander and his wife; even some of the women ignore her who used to be her friend, they pretended she doesn't exist. They never speak to her, even though she has tried.

She was happy now for the first time in many, many years, and it was all because of Paul. He tells her ten times a day just how much he loves her, and he shows it with every touch and caress. He does things for her to make her feel special, and she loves him, something she never thought she would be able to do again.

She had learned that love is unconditional; it has no limitations. It gives you confidence to dream and to share your hopes and deepest, darkest secrets to. That someone special you have always waited for. Love is unexpected, and it assures you that you are not alone in the world and that someone will always put you first. True love is vulnerable, and it can break you and tear your heart into tiny pieces. But to be deeply loved by someone gives you courage, strength, and happiness to move forward in life. Love is invisible, and only the heart can see it. Love is putting someone else's happiness before yours. She had learned that love is magic and that there is no greater happiness in life than to have someone to love and something to hope for.

"I hope that I never fall under another man's influence to do what they tell me. But one thing is for certain, no man will ever hurt me again, not physically, mentally or verbally. I am happy with whom I have become. I'm no longer afraid to stay locked in my room, or say what I think."

"I write about the power of trying, because I want to be okay with failure. I write about generosity because I battle the people who dislike. I write about joy because I know sorrow. I write about faith because I almost lost mine and I know what it is to be broken and in need of redemption. I write about gratitude because I am thankful for all of it."

"I have suffered failure, loneliness, sorrow, discouragement, and death- but God will conquer all these horrors and evil. But through it all I still know that just to be alive is God's will."

Page of Love and Hate

Maggie sometimes wishes that she could turn back the clock and have the courage then that she does now. She knows in her heart that she would have left David and not waited for the children to become adults. Because she still thinks of how close she came to being killed by him that night, and it was only by the grace of God that she was alive.

Carol Bryant

KEYWORDS

OCEAN, BEACH, SEA, SUNRISE, SUNSET

Printed in the USA
CPSIA information can be obtained
at www.ICGtesting.com
LVHW020207130424
777223LV00011B/201